Praise f

J

Heaven Sent: Heaven

"I absolutely loved the way Jet Mykles challenges the reader to look beyond the typical black and white and ask questions of themselves even as the characters are doing so."

—Maura Anderson, *The Romance Studio*

Heaven Sent: Purgatory

"*Purgatory* is quite simply everything I wanted it to be: tender, romantic, sexy and immensely satisfying."

—Shannon, *Joyfully Reviewed*

Tech Support

"This is a strong romance with steamy sex scenes that will leave you breathless and wanting more."

—Robin, *Romance Junkies*

Leashed: Two for One Deal

"The humor and quick discourse alone made this a fantastic story, yet with the combination of three awesome characters and steamy sex scenes an erotic reader could not ask for anything more in a story."

—Marina, *Cupid's Library Reviews*

Leashed: More Than a Bargain

"Jet Mykles is making her presence known in the world of the erotic paranormal romance with this masterpiece. Without a doubt, *More Than a Bargain* is a 5 star, homerun work."

—Kimberly Spinney, *eCataromance*

These titles are all available in ebook format at Loose Id®.

LooseId ®

ISBN 10: 1-59632-456-2
ISBN 13: 978-1-59632-456-5
LEASHED: MORE THAN A BARGAIN
Copyright © 2006 by Jet Mykles
Originally released in e-book format in October 2006

Cover Art by April Martinez

Printed in the U.S.A. by
Lightning Source, Inc.
1246 Heil Quaker Blvd
La Vergne TN 37086
www.lightningsource.com

LEASHED:
MORE THAN A BARGAIN

Jet Mykles

Chapter One

My cell phone rang. I picked it up from the little table beside the plush recliner in which I sat and glanced at the display. It was Gwen. I flipped it open. "Hey."

"Hey. What's up?"

I smiled, aiming the remote at the television and clicking the mute button. I wasn't really into the cop drama anyway. "Nothing. Watching TV."

"How ordinary."

"I know. What's up with you?"

"Eating dinner. Mac and cheese."

"Healthy."

"Filling." She paused and I figured she was chewing. "So where are *they?*"

I grimaced a bit at the emphasis on "they." I'm pretty sure she was a bit ticked that I had not one but two lovers now, when only last week I had none. "Outside. Full moon and all."

"I thought that was a myth?"

"No. It's a myth that shifters *have* to change on the full moon. They don't. But the moon does call to them, and most will go out for the night." I giggled. "I knew some shifters in New York who'd go clubbing full-moon night. I'm told it was a wild time."

Gwen halfheartedly matched my giggle. "That must be something."

"I'm told it is. My sisters *loved* to go out when it was a full moon."

"Not you?"

"Please. You know me, Gwen; I'm not much into the clubbing scene."

"You're not at *all* into the clubbing scene, despite my best efforts." She sighed. "So, where do your guys live? There must be some heavy-duty land out there if Michael's running around as a jaguar."

"Oh, it's gorgeous. There are trees everywhere, and there's this ridge not far away that looks out over the mountain slope. Michael and Rudy say there are deer, but I didn't see any when they took me up there the other day."

"Mmm." The clanking of dishes over the line signaled that Gwen had finished eating. "So, how are you? Really. For the past few days I don't get much more than an 'I'm fine'; then one or the other of your shifters pulls you off the phone. Usually to have sex."

I heard the disdain in the last sentence even though I recognized that she was trying to control it. If Gwen was really set on being a bitch, she'd just lay into me. I settled a bit deeper into my nest in the recliner, pulling the afghan over my knees and up under my breasts. I wasn't really cold, even though I only wore thin sweatpants, a T-shirt, and socks, but the afghan was snuggly and smelled faintly of Michael and Rudy. A wood-burning stove in the corner of the room worked beautifully for keeping out the chill. Turning my gaze toward the big, sliding glass door on the left, I stared at my reflection. By day, the door looked over the backyard and the trees beyond. But right now, by the measly light of one lamp and the television, the glass was a mirror showing me curled up under a light, crocheted afghan in the depths of the maroon recliner. I looked very small. "I'm okay."

"That's the same thing as 'I'm fine.' God, Meg, talk to me."

I picked at the yarn of the afghan. What did she want me to say? *I killed a man the other night. I sapped all his power and most, if not all, of his memories and left his body an empty husk. Now I need these two shapeshifters that I barely know to help me keep control of more power than I can handle and memories that aren't mine. I haven't got a clue what that'll do to me in the long run, but I'm sure it's bad.* Although it was the truth, I couldn't say any of that to Gwen. She was my best friend, but there were things she just didn't need to know. And I'd paused too long. "There's nothing to tell."

"Nothing."

"Nothing."

"I don't believe you."

"I'm sorry."

I heard a sighing growl, then a long pause. Pauses in Gwen's speech were never a good thing. It meant there were things she really wanted to say but wouldn't because she didn't want to upset me. "The news says that Roland Parks died of a heart attack."

I kept my voice as bland as I could. "Yes, it does."

"Not an animal attack."

"You know the local press covers up any evidence of shifters." All major press did, thanks to the enforcers. Michael had told me he'd called them. The enforcers were what equated to the paranormal authorities. Local representatives of the Witches' Council, as well as the enforcers, would have been all over the scene not long after we'd left it, removing or disguising any evidence of magical doings.

But no one would find evidence of an animal attack. Not on Roland Parks, that is. Neither Michael nor Rudy had laid a claw on him. His death was all *my* doing. I'd yet to find out what either group of authorities—shifter or human—thought of the empty husk of a man they'd found. They might not have realized what happened. He was dead, after all. His soul departed. It wasn't farfetched for his memories and power to have drained away with his passing of sorts. The authorities couldn't know exactly which spells he'd used just before his death. He *had* been trying to cast a spell to bring me completely under his control. I had to defend myself, right?

"We shouldn't talk about this over the phone," I reminded her.

"You don't give me much choice since you haven't come in to the shop. Or by my place." If her voice had been a whip, I'd have had welts.

I winced. "I'm sorry. It's been…I just needed some time after Halloween."

"Uh-huh. So you're feeling better? Rested?"

Five days since I'd left her at our bookshop to go off in the company of my newly leashed shifters. It had been four days since Halloween. Four days since Roland had forcibly taken me to his manor and I eventually killed him. It seemed like a lifetime.

"Yeah. I think I'm okay now."

"Okay enough to come in to the shop?"

Together Gwen and I owned a small bookshop/internet café. We catered to witches, but we had mundane customers as well. The latter just didn't know about the former. We'd had the shop for almost two years. It didn't make us rich, but it often made us happy.

"I…don't know."

She pushed out an exasperated breath. "Meg, I need you to come in tomorrow."

"Is anything wrong?"

"Yes, actually. It's after the first of the month, and I don't know how to pay the bills."

I nearly dropped the phone. "Oh, shit! Gwen, I'd forgotten all about that!"

"Yeah. I kind of figured."

"I'm so sorry."

"So, you'll come in tomorrow?"

Instinct told me not to, but I had responsibilities. "Yes."

"You sure?"

I squeezed my eyes shut. "Gwen, I'm sorry. I know I flaked on you and that's unforgivable. But I won't jeopardize the store. I'll be there tomorrow."

"Good." I heard the relief in her voice. "I mean, I know you've been through a lot, but we can't afford the late fees."

"I know."

Pause. "Meg?"

"Yeah?"

"I'm here for you. You know that, right? If you want to talk about it?"

I bit my lip. "I know that."

"I just…" Her voice softened. "Roland's dead, honey. He can't hurt you anymore."

Wanna bet? I put my hand over my eyes, but it didn't stop the tears. "I know that."

"Okay. Okay. I should get to bed, then. Unless there's something else?"

I glanced at the clock. Nine p.m. Not near Gwen's bedtime. She was letting me off the phone. "No. There's nothing."

"Okay. If you say so. I'll see you tomorrow."

"Right. See you tomorrow."

I flipped my cell phone closed and stared at it. I wished I could tell her what was happening. I could use another outlook on certain things. But even though Gwen was a witch, she was both a very new witch and a very weak one. She barely had enough in her to cast some of the simpler spells. But she was more sensitive to magic than many witches I'd met, so I'd been teaching her things. Just little things. Enough so that she knew she wasn't crazy for seeing or feeling things that mundanes didn't.

Sighing, I turned to put my cell phone on the table beside the chair and twisted to reach for the remote.

And saw him. The jaguar sat calmly in the darkened doorway to the hall at the far end of the room. The lack of light blended the darkness behind him with the black of his pelt, making him nearly invisible except for the sheen on his fur. His green eyes, however, glowed in the faint illumination from the television. They were trained steadily on me. His tail wound about his legs, the end twitching slightly.

I jumped. I hadn't felt him come into the house. I hadn't been aware he was near at all. How had he snuck up on me? The metaphysical leash that bound him to me should've warned me of his proximity.

I sent a mental tug briefly on Rudy's leash, checking it. I felt him, still outside, far enough away from the house that it would take him at least a few minutes to get to me if I called him back. I couldn't tell what he was physically doing, but I knew he was enjoying himself. Enjoying the night. He paused and sent a questioning thought to me. It wasn't words, just feeling. I sent soothing thoughts his way and did the equivalent of shaking my head, letting him know there was no emergency to hurry back for.

Meanwhile, I stared into Michael's green eyes. Why hadn't I felt him? I mentally probed toward him and felt him, barely. He'd done something to mask his presence. Sort of like taking your shoes off to tiptoe up on someone. If I'd been listening or paying attention, I'd have felt him. But I hadn't, so he'd snuck up on me on purpose. I hadn't known shifters could do that.

"How long have you been sitting there?"

He stood and stepped toward me in one fluid, feline motion. The kind of motion that made you wonder if there were any bones at all in the cat's body, or if it was all flexing, powerful muscle. Once the tip of his tail passed the threshold, his body disappeared in a flash of what wasn't quite light, to be replaced a second later by his naked human form. Like his cat form, Michael's body was all fluid, muscular grace. He kept walking toward me, as though he hadn't just been on all fours a brief moment before. "You're not going in to the shop tomorrow."

I blinked, distracted by the sight of satin skin with fine, sparse hair over acres of hard, male muscle. Of my two lovers, Michael was just more *male*. Not that Rudy wasn't all man, but Michael just exuded what you'd think of when you think "masculine." Sleek black hair rivaling his cat-form pelt fell from the top of his head to just past his shoulders. One heavy lock threatened to obscure his right eye. His face was all hard, blunted lines, which made him look slightly feline in this form as well. His eyes were pure emerald green.

I blinked again when he came to a stop at my side, belatedly processing what he'd said. "What?"

"You heard me. You can't go out in public. It's too dangerous."

I fought the distraction of gazing at his body by focusing on his eyes. The fact that they were serious, almost angry, and not their usual heatedly seductive helped me to concentrate. "I'm not going out in public. I'm going to the shop."

He rolled his eyes. "It amounts to the same thing."

"No, it doesn't."

"Yes, it does."

I frowned. "I don't see what the big deal is."

He glowered, then turned and stomped across the room—well, his equivalent of a stomp, which was still silent and graceful. It was more of an angry-stomp feeling to his movement. He crossed between me and the silent television to the sliding glass door. "Meg, I don't want to have this conversation again."

I crossed my arms over my chest, telling myself that I was *not* catching a glance at his fine, tight ass or that broad, mouth-watering back. "Excuse me, but who exactly gave you the right to boss me around?"

He twisted just the upper half of his body and pointed at me. "*You* did, the moment you first leashed me."

I pulled my bottom lip back in when I realized I was pouting. "I seem to recall that the last leashing was by request."

"It's the first one that counts." He turned back to slide open the door.

I narrowed my eyes at him. Again, *not* checking out his ass, no matter how finely it flexed as he moved. "Whatever. It still doesn't give you the right to deny my going in to work."

He faced me again, arms crossed over his chest. Of course, now I had to not notice his cock, which, even completely unaroused, was a sight to behold. "Oh? How do you propose to get there?"

When they'd brought me to their house, we'd left my car at the shop. It was still sitting there. Other than a nearly disastrous trip to the home of a megalomaniacal witch who'd wanted to own me, I'd not been away from their house in the hills.

I glared. "So you propose to keep me prisoner here?"

He sighed, shaking his head. One hand came up to pinch the bridge of his nose. "I'm trying to *protect* you. That's what you called me to do."

"Good Goddess, Michael. Roland's dead! What is there to protect me *from?*"

I heard the distinct click of canine claws on the cemented patio outside. I felt Rudy's nearness even if I still couldn't see him in the night.

Michael dropped his hand back to cross the arm over his chest. His face was deadly serious, black brows crowded down over his green eyes. "Yes, Roland is dead. And you harbor most, if not all, of his memories. And power. Both of which tend to surface at strange times."

I watched the tawny wolf nose through the opening in the door, rather than see the weight of Michael's stare. "I was fine today."

"One day without any mishaps, with only me and Rudy around. We don't know what will happen when you're around other people."

The wolf's crystal-blue gaze darted from me to Michael and back again. He then disappeared in a flash, and Rudy's human form appeared, all tall, lean, and naked, with only his sunny brown hair as a resemblance to his canine form. Well, and a slight wolfish cast to his features, but that could be my projecting his personality in my vision of him. He put his hands on his hips, flexing biceps ringed with black tribal tattoos. "What happened now?"

Michael and I said nothing.

Rudy rolled his eyes, reaching back to shut the sliding glass door and lock it. His own trim little ass flexed as he moved. "Someone please fill me in."

"She wants to go in to work tomorrow."

I tore my eyes from Rudy's derriere, dropping my traitorous gaze to my lap. Looking at the oodles of male goodness before me wasn't helping me win this argument. Time for another tactic. "It's not a matter of want, Michael. I really need to. It's after the first of the month, and we've got to pay bills."

"Gwen can't do it?" Rudy asked.

"No, she can't. She's hopeless with our accounting program. She can count up daily totals, but she can't pay the monthly bills."

"What would she do if you got sick or something?"

I scowled, threading my fingers through the holes in the afghan draped over my knees. "She'd have a problem. And before you ask, yes, I *have* gone in sick to do the bills."

"You need an accountant," Michael declared.

"Can't afford one."

"I'll get you one."

My heart skipped. "Generous of you, but I'd still have to go in, wouldn't I?"

He humphed. "It's a bad idea."

I resisted the urge to look up at either of them. "If we don't pay the bills, we risk losing the store, Michael."

"What if you lose control?" Michael asked blandly. "We can't very well fuck you in public. Or is that what you're hoping?"

I blushed, untangling my fingers from the afghan. Unfortunately, he was right. Well, not about my wanting it. About that being the only way to put me back in control of myself. When Roland's memories overwhelmed me over the last few days, only sex with one or the other—or both—of them had brought me back to myself. And not just sex, but hardcore, bang-me-so-hard-that-I-still-felt-it-days-later sex. I squirmed at the mere thought, my pussy starting to moisten. Goddess, in the last week, I'd had exponentially more sex than I'd had in the past twenty-six years of my life, and just the thought of it made me want more. I was hopeless, but now was not the time. "I won't lose control. I was fine today." There, my voice sounded steady.

"You haven't had any control over it yet."

"I'll be fine."

Michael sighed. I saw his feet approach me out of the corner of my eyes. "Meg…"

I snapped my gaze back to him, halting him in his tracks. "We need to find out sometime."

He scowled at me, then changed his direction, stalking between me and the television across the room once again. "We do. But not like this." He left through the darkened opening into the depths of the house.

I exchanged looks with Rudy. He hadn't moved once as he watched us. Monitoring us. Blue eyes shone from behind a thick fringe of light brown hair. He stood casually, but that long, leanly muscled body of his always looked like it was wound tight and ready to spring.

"What's your take on this?"

He dragged a hand through his hair, drawing my attention to the stretch of his lovely chest. "I dunno, Meg. One day's not really much, and those memories are pretty bad."

I grimaced, more upset because he was right. They were both right. Didn't take away the fact that I had to go in. Or that it was now a matter of principle. Michael simply could *not* dictate my life!

In a huff, I kicked out, intending to send the afghan flying over my knees to the floor. It didn't work out that way. One of my bare toes hooked through part of the afghan, and one of the holes snagged on the metal extension thing connecting the recliner with its footrest. I ended up struggling with a tangle around my legs and chair.

Rudy stepped up and knelt to helpfully unhook the blanket from the recliner. As soon as I could kick my legs free, I scrambled to my feet.

"Meg."

I heard Rudy, but didn't look back, already at the opening to the hallway, following Michael. He was the one I needed to convince. We all knew that.

I stomped down the darkened hallway, following the feel of him to the master bedroom. Now that I was paying attention, he couldn't mask the leash.

A second wood-burning stove stood at the end of the hall, providing warmth for this end of the long ranch house. The red fire behind the little door at its bottom was a beacon in the inky darkness. I reached the bedroom and slammed my hand into the light switch, flooding the room with light.

Michael sat calmly on the edge of the bed, one leg folded on the mattress and one trailing over the side. He faced the door. Waiting.

Bastard.

I stopped a few steps into the room. "Why not? Why can't I go in and test out my control?"

"You'll put your friend in danger."

"Gwen?"

"Yes."

"I wouldn't hurt Gwen!"

He cocked his head to the side, letting silky black hair skim over his shoulders. "And before a few days ago, would you have killed someone?"

My hands fisted. "Oh, fuck you! That's a low blow."

"But it's true."

Tears sprang to my eyes, blurring my vision. I bit my lip on a sob that choked my throat. I had no words to throw back at him because he was completely and absolutely right. The only reason I'd leashed Michael and Rudy in the first place had been to save myself from Roland Parks, a burgeoning grand wizard with designs on owning me and the magical gifts I was born with.

Their help had worked. We'd defeated Roland rather successfully. *Too* successfully. I'd lost control in the end and had not only killed Roland with my magic—an offense punishable by death if it could be proven by the Witches' Council—but also drained *his* magic—an even worse crime. I'd effectively stolen his power. But I don't think the memories I'd acquired were part of what normally happened when a witch stole another's power. I'd done something wrong. Something profoundly frightening. Only the fact that I was intimately bound—physically and metaphysically—to Michael and Rudy saved me, and only the fact that Michael seemed to know *way* too much about magic for a shifter got us to be that close, that fast. Using my link with them, I'd managed to spread the power and memories among us, borrowing their strength. I was the only one who was visited by the memories or experienced the surges of power, but they were my conduits and my grounding. Without them, I would have imploded from sheer energy overload.

A comforting set of arms slid around me from behind. Rudy nuzzled my neck, one arm encircling my ribs below my breasts and the other banded about my shoulders just under my throat. Warm breath caressed my ear. "Give it a few more days, Meg." The fact that no erection poked my backside told me that he was unhappy with the argument.

Well, I wasn't *happy* with the argument. I'd like nothing better than to just enjoy them both, get a good night's sleep, then go in to work the next day. But Michael was being so hardheaded! "I can't." A sob cracked in my voice. "It's my responsibility. It's after the first of the month, and the bills have to be paid. That's my job."

Michael shook his head, leaning back, bracing brawny arms on the mattress. "Meg, the fact remains that it's too dangerous. You could lose control at any moment."

I broke from Rudy's embrace, certain that I'd completely break down if I allowed it to continue. I stopped a few steps in front of Michael's knees. "Look, Michael, I was pretty sketchy right after Halloween. I'll admit that. I needed to recover. Yes, it's scary. But I was *fine* today. Nothing will happen."

Green eyes searched my face. "Who are you trying to convince?"

I tried not to grind my teeth, but was only partially successful. I did manage not to stomp my foot, but I couldn't stop the tears that fell down my cheeks. "This is my *life* we're talking about."

He frowned, showing only a fraction of anger compared to mine. "Yes. It is. A life that Rudy and I are bound to protect. So let me do what you called me to do."

"I don't need protection."

"Don't you?"

"I got away from my mother to escape all that shit. I've lived away from her for five years without anything happening."

"You've been lucky."

I threw up my hands. Unable to look at him and the deadly-serious stare he wore, I started to pace. "You're blowing this *way* out of proportion. Who would want me now that Roland's dead?"

Rudy braced his butt against the heavy oak dresser across one wall, arms folded, monitoring us again.

"Do you think that Roland was the only one of his kind?" The mild anger faded from Michael's voice, and he dropped back further on the mattress, leaning on his elbows. The vivid green of the top sheet, the only covering on the bed, framed him beautifully. The position made his broad chest look even bigger. It also presented his nice fat cock to advantage. I knew it'd be warm, fragrant, and delicious if I let myself go to him to touch it.

I avoided looking at him.

"Think again, sweetheart. There are plenty of witches out there who'll want you once they find out about you."

"No one knows about me!"

"No? How did Roland find out?"

"I don't know."

"And *that* is cause enough for concern. He found you and had enough skill to tame you."

Forgetting that I didn't want to look at him, I rounded, hands on hips. "He didn't tame—!"

He raised his voice, barreling over my protest. "He was damn near close! If you hadn't called Rudy and me, even with your instinctive power, you'd be toast. Even *with* us, it was a close thing, and you know it. If I had been like most shifters and not known the first thing about magic, you'd be Roland's right now."

Just because it was true didn't make it any easier for me to swallow. I avoided the matter of his unusual knowledge of magic. That was a topic for another time. I went back to pacing.

"Gwen can't handle the store by herself anymore," I grumbled. "There are bills to pay, and she's hopeless at it."

"You've mentioned that about a dozen times."

"But you don't seem to be *understanding* what I'm saying."

"I understand just fine," he snapped.

"Can you do any of it remotely?" Rudy suggested helpfully.

I turned and stopped, eyeing him from across the room. "No. Not all of it. I need the actual pieces of paper."

He shrugged. "Maybe she can bring them to you after work tomorrow?"

"Good idea. What's more important?" Michael asked. "The shop or your life?"

I glared at Michael, doing, I think, a good imitation of his snarl. "Damn it!" Fully aware I was being petulant, I stormed into the bathroom and shut the door. I didn't bother running water. They knew I was giving myself time to think. Or, if they didn't, it didn't matter.

I leaned on the sink, staring at myself. Big brown eyes glared back at me. I tried to see what attracted them. It couldn't just be physical. I don't think that I'm bad-looking, but I'm no raving beauty. Thanks to a very pale-skinned mother and a very dark-skinned father, I have skin that's a rather nice shade of cocoa. My hair is long, straight, and on a good day, glossy almost-black. On a less-than-good day, a dull dark brown. My face is round, my eyes wide-spaced, and I think that my nose is a tad too broad and flat, although that's not really overstated.

Nope, it wasn't just physical. There was something about me. Something in my power that attracted them. Whether they were actually conscious of it, who knew? They probably weren't. But whatever it was, they were willing to protect me. Willing to put their lives on the line. They'd already done so, once. They'd already shown a willingness to share the weight of unnatural power on my shoulders. They were the first in my life to offer such support. It felt good. It felt warm. It felt scary as hell.

My life was trickling away, becoming something I'd left New York to avoid. I came from one of the top families of witches; my mother was the grand dame of Northeast United States. I'd run from the dubious prestige of being the sixth daughter of a seventh daughter of a seventh daughter, etcetera, back to the 1200s. I craved a life of anonymity. I didn't want to be a mundane, but I'd love a life where magic was an aid rather than a ruling principle. Keeping Michael and Rudy didn't ensure that I'd live that kind of life.

I finally turned on the water and used it to wash the tears from my face and brush my teeth. Grimly, I ran a brush through my hair, then headed out.

They sat on the bed, talking quietly. Michael was propped up on pillows piled against the headboard, legs spread before him. Rudy sat cross-legged in the middle of the mattress, between Michael's feet. As I entered, he immediately rolled onto his knees, facing me. Disheveled, golden-brown hair covered one of his clear blue, concerned eyes. The fact that he wasn't aroused meant that they really had been talking and not just amusing themselves while they waited. Michael turned, directing a sullen stare at me from beneath silky black bangs.

I stared at them. Two gorgeous men with whom I'd slept repeatedly in the last few days. With whom I now shared frighteningly strong metaphysical bonds. If I skewed my vision just a bit, I'd be able to see the orange glow of the leashes I'd put on them, circling their necks and the bases of their cocks. Those leashes were magically bound to me, rooted deep in my heart and in my womb. Despite the visual feast, despite the fact that the magic made them mine, my unenviable stubborn streak rose with a vengeance. I turned and stalked toward the door.

"Where are you going?" Michael's mild voice reached my ears.

"I'm not sleeping in here tonight."

I heard the bed creak as Rudy bounded off it. "What?"

I turned at the door, my hand out, palm facing him.

He stopped, a look of total confusion twisting his adorable face. He spread his hands. "Meg, come on…"

"No." I looked at Michael, knowing if I gazed too long into Rudy's pleading eyes, I'd give.

Michael remained where he was, arms crossed, watching us. He cocked his head, his lips a line of disgust. "Stop being childish."

Which just pissed me off more. "I'm not being childish!" Oh, yeah, that proved my point.

He rolled his eyes and turned, scooting to the edge of the bed.

"Stay where you are."

He stood. "No."

All six-foot-five of brawny, muscular maleness sauntered toward me. My skin tingled, anticipating his touch. I knew it so well now, *craved* it almost. Those green eyes fastened on me, and damned if my belly didn't flip. Out of the corner of my eye, I saw his cock start to twitch to life. The tingle between my legs told me that my pussy noticed.

I pointed at him, ignoring my body's response. Just because it was there didn't mean I had to give in. "I mean it, Michael. I'm not sleeping with you two tonight."

"Why not?" Goddess, that purr!

I backed a step into the hallway.

An uncertain look in his eye, Rudy glanced back as Michael advanced. "Mike…"

Michael paid him no heed, his attention on me. He reached for my arm as he passed Rudy's shoulder. "Come here, Meg. We'll make you forget all about work."

"Fuck you!"

It was childish and petty, but I did it anyway. I reached inside and yanked at the leash around his neck.

His eyes went big as he staggered backwards. His legs actually gave out, and he toppled to the carpet, arms out to catch himself. It was amazingly ungraceful, especially for him. Evidently, I'd tugged a little harder than intended. I had less control over my magic when I was pissed.

I backed to the far wall of the hallway, but Rudy dashed out the door and caught my arm. "Meg, wait."

I dropped my gaze and concentrated on the black tribal tattoo that banded his right bicep, rather than look into those beautiful blue eyes. Even if they were in shadow, I knew them too well now, and the hurt in them would be my undoing. "Let go." I jerked my head toward the guest bedroom. "I'm sleeping in there tonight."

"But, Meg—Hey!" Rudy stumbled back, hand falling from my arm.

I looked up.

Michael was on his feet and stood behind Rudy, hands on his shoulders. The tension in Michael's fingers showed me he was holding Rudy back.

Rudy frowned over his shoulder, up at Michael.

Michael stared at me, nostrils flaring only slightly. His face was blank as he slid one hand down Rudy's shoulder, spanning his palm and fingers over one of Rudy's pecs. "Stay." It wasn't exactly a command, more of a heavy request.

I shook my head. Even though my body creamed in a natural reaction to all the delicious manflesh available to me, my mind wouldn't let me enjoy it. It was the principle of the thing. I wouldn't allow him to command me.

Rudy reached out a hand. "Meg..."

I tore my gaze from him and entered the guest room. Neither of them followed me.

Chapter Two

I crawled under the thick blue comforter with my T-shirt and sweats still on. A first for the past few days. Clothes had definitely been unnecessary and unwelcome when climbing into bed. I'd slept in the second bedroom exactly once since I'd been there. One nap after a long shower. A nap that had been interrupted when Rudy had come to carry me to the master bedroom. I hadn't gotten back to sleep for a few hours after that, but it was an enjoyable interlude. Sex with those two had yet to be anything but enjoyable. Explosive. Rock-your-world kind of sex. Always wonderful, often intense, sometimes downright scary. I'd just gotten used to the various aches over the past few days. Not that I *minded* so much.

Damn! I missed them. What the hell was wrong with me? Sex wasn't the end-all, be-all. I could spend *one* night without some thick part of some hot male body filling one or more of my body's orifices.

Sleep, however, eluded me. I tossed and turned and tried various different positions. I fought to keep my eyes closed, but nothing worked. I was wide awake. And there was nothing to cause it except the absence of the two bodies that I'd shared space with the last few nights. I was uncomfortable despite the warm, soft bed. I was irritated. I was...aroused?

I stared at the indigo shadows of the ceiling, confused. What the hell? But there was no getting around it. My nipples were hard points, scraping against the inside of my T-shirt. My skin was tingling as though from caresses. My pussy was so wet that either one of my well-endowed lovers could have easily slid inside. They could do this to me when they weren't there? But that didn't make sense. I'd been apart from them before. I'd taken a few short naps without them and slept just fine without this itchy, antsy feeling. Was it because I'd walked away from them? Or was it...

Suddenly I wasn't seeing the ceiling of the guest bedroom. My entire focus turned inward. I wouldn't say that I could *see* them exactly, but I abruptly knew what Michael and Rudy were doing and knew it was the cause of my distress.

They were fucking, and the leashes allowed me along for the ride. This had happened before, but I'd been with them at the time, not a complete outsider.

I felt Michael's mouth wrapped around Rudy's cock. Not as if it were my own. More of a reflection of the pleasure that made Rudy clutch at the mattress and clench his eyes shut, panting softly. I felt the echoes of Michael's intensity as he sucked his lover, holding Rudy's thighs down to prevent him from pumping. I sensed Michael pressing his own erection into the mattress, torturing himself with the inadequate attempt at relief.

I turned over, staring blindly at the darkened wall. Moans started escaping Rudy's throat, still too soft for me to actually hear from the other room, but the sentiment was plenty loud in my head. I closed my eyes, then snapped them back open when the intensity of their feelings threatened to drown me. I curled my hands into the pillow beneath my head in a desperate attempt to avoid touching the soaking wetness between my thighs. It felt wrong, somehow. This was their time together. They'd been lovers long before I'd come into the picture. Although they both attested to my welcome, I still felt like the third wheel.

Rudy's orgasm ramped closer, eclipsing my sense of Michael. My hips fought against invisible hands, mirroring Rudy's vain attempt to shove down Michael's throat. He threw his head back, hissing Michael's name over and over as pleasure grabbed hold and yanked a shuddering climax out of him.

I scooted toward the edge of the bed, intending to get up and walk around. Anything to distract myself from what I was feeling. I nearly collapsed when I got there, overcome as Rudy's echoed pleasure again took me over. Fingers in his ass, a sensation that I personally was still getting used to, but one that Rudy found amazingly erotic. The fact that they were Michael's fingers only made it better for him. I rode his pleasure for agonizing minutes, twitching and biting down on a moan that almost echoed his own.

That was it! I had to see!

Gathering what I could of my wits, I slipped out of bed. I left the guest bedroom and crossed the hall to their door. Closed. It hadn't been closed during the entire time that I'd been in the house. I stood there, feeling like a pervert for wanting to watch them. From there, I heard Rudy's soft cries, even as I felt the echo of what caused it.

My hand dropped to the doorknob and twisted. The door swung out of the way just as Michael sank his cock deep into Rudy's body. The angle didn't allow me to see it, but I could feel the echo of it. They'd left the light on, so I could see Michael's broad back and tight ass. Rudy's legs bracketed that back, hands hooked underneath his knees to hold them up and apart. Michael leaned forward between them, bracing his hands on the mattress.

Unable to help myself, I slid into the room, crabbing sideways until I could see them both in profile. I'd never known that the missionary position was possible for men. The angle just didn't seem right. But now that I saw it, it seemed perfect. Neither one of them was complaining or uncomfortable.

They were beautiful to watch, two big, muscled bodies locked in love, sliding easily together thanks to the sweat sheening their skin. Rudy released his legs to reach up and encircle Michael's neck. He urged his lover further down until they were chest to chest and took Michael's lips in a wet, avid kiss. Michael caught Rudy's knee, hooking it over his elbow as he continued a steady, pulsing rhythm deep into Rudy's body. It opened Rudy up to me so I could clearly see Michael's gleaming wet cock sliding in and out of Rudy's body.

Moans grew in volume. They knew I was there. Had I been anyone else, they would've stopped. There was no sneaking up on shifters, even if they were engrossed in each other. They knew I was there and they didn't mind. Or they didn't care.

This time pleasure buffeted me from both of them. Both men fought toward orgasm with single-minded intensity. Rudy clutched Michael's shoulders and Michael braced up on his arms, the better to pound into the man beneath him. When they came, it was like a two tidal waves crashing into me, first Rudy, then Michael. Overwhelmed, I collapsed against the wall, sliding down it when my knees buckled beneath me.

They stayed joined for precious moments, each panting hard. Rudy pulled Michael's head down for another kiss, this one slow, sensuous, and seemingly endless.

Their emotions released me. My body still hummed, mentally but not physically satisfied. As they kissed, I shoved to my feet. I went to the bathroom and grabbed two washcloths, ran the water until it was warm, and soaked both of them. After wringing them out enough so that they didn't drip, I grabbed one of the big towels that hung beside the shower and re-entered the bedroom.

Michael was on his knees between Rudy's splayed thighs, hands in his sweaty hair to push it back. Rudy lay like a limp noodle before him, a happy, sated grin on his shining, lush lips. They both turned to me when I stopped at the side of the bed. I offered a washcloth to Michael. After a brief pause, he took it. Ever the considerate lover, he reached down to clean up Rudy first.

"Meg." Rudy's soft utterance went straight to my heart. When he stretched out a hand toward me, I had to go to him. I knelt on the bed, carefully setting the remaining wet cloth on his belly, then bent over to place a soft kiss on those swollen lips. He caught the hair at the side of my head, keeping me close when I would have pulled back. "Stay."

Rudy's soft entreaty moved me where Michael's earlier veiled command had not. When he pulled me into a proper kiss, I went. Braced on one elbow on the mattress beside his shoulder and a hand splayed in the sweat and semen on his chest, I kissed him with a slight edge of desperation. I *wanted* to be there with them. I wanted to feel like I could watch them. I wanted them to be free to have each other. I wanted to share my body freely with them and enjoy theirs in return.

Why the hell did real life have to get in the way?

As I couldn't see him, I couldn't completely decipher Michael's movements. I moved my hand when he nudged it and figured that he was using the other wet cloth to wipe down Rudy's chest. A jar of the mattress told me when he left the bed. He moved away enough, at least, for Rudy to turn over and reach for my shirt to try and tug it off.

I pulled back, catching his hands. "No. Stop."

"Oh come on, Meg. Let me…"

"Don't force her, Rudy."

We both twisted to look at Michael, who stood beside the bed drying his hair with the big towel I'd brought. The two wet washcloths were in his other hand. "We've already found out that she doesn't respond well to it."

I glared at his back as he went to the bathroom. I opened my mouth to throw a response at him, but Rudy cut me off. Quick as a wink, he tackled me to the bed, rolling on top of me.

"Rudy, stop."

"Okay, okay. Calm down. I won't do anything." He caught my gaze, his own earnest. "But stay with us the rest of the night."

"He doesn't want me here."

"Yeah, he does. Goddess, you both are so stubborn!" He lowered his head to nuzzle my neck. In a voice too low for even Michael's sensitive ears to hear, he said, "We'll convince him to let you go to the shop in the morning. I promise. Just stay." He kissed my neck.

"Rudy."

He nibbled my jaw. "Please, Meg."

"You two should have some time alone."

"We've had time alone." His lips made it to mine. "Now it's time for you to join us."

I got lost in our kiss. The warm, drugging taste of his lips and tongue. The man made an art form of kissing, switching nibbling and sucking at all the right times to make sure I stayed involved.

The feel of the mattress sinking to the side of us jerked me out of it. Rudy rolled off me like he'd planned it, landing in his accustomed spot on the bed. I watched Michael situate himself to my other side. Our eyes met, and I couldn't tell what he was thinking. Would he throw me out? Would he say some egotistical, typically male remark that would force me to leave again?

But he said nothing. He plumped his pillow into submission, then sank his head into it, closing his eyes. On my other side, Rudy rolled onto his belly, hugging his own pillow and facing away from me. I stared at the ceiling a moment, thinking I should go. This was getting way too intense. I was being swallowed up and I wasn't sure that I liked it. Forget that it was my spell that had called them to me in the first place.

But it was warm. The smell of sex, even though it hadn't involved me, was oddly comforting. With a sigh, I turned and put my back to Michael. My arm slid around Rudy's waist, and I rested my cheek on the back of one of his shoulders. The scent of sweaty male and fresh sex filled my senses and didn't remotely upset me.

Just as I was drifting off to sleep, I felt Michael adjusting. His arm landed softly across my waist and his thigh curled up under mine.

Chapter Three

I woke to lips caressing the sensitive skin just behind my ear. I blinked sleepily, my blurry vision filled with the golden, tanned expanse of Rudy's smooth back. I felt him twitching. Turning my gaze downward, I saw Michael's arm across my hips, his hand buried and busy between Rudy's thighs.

My shirt was pushed up under my armpits and my sweats were down around my knees, just far enough out of the way to bare my ass so Michael could insert his cock between my thighs. Waking further, I now felt him hard as stone, the tip of him massaging my clit as he moved. His weight pushed me into Rudy, crushing my breasts against his back.

Rudy moaned, clutching the sheet beneath him. I couldn't tell if he was awake or not, but I figured he would be soon enough.

Teeth bit down gently on the back of my shoulder and I groaned. It hurt because he was biting a healing wound, but it was his bite in the first place, so it was strangely erotic. I snuggled closer to Rudy's back to get some relief for my nipples, while rocking my hips back, clutching my thighs tight for Michael.

Michael's hand took the one I had splayed across Rudy's side and pulled it down to wrap around Rudy's damp cock. "Take over for me."

Happily, I complied, loving the feel of Rudy hot and hard in my hand. I pumped him, making sure to finger just underneath the head, where I knew he liked it most. I was rewarded with a tortured moan.

Michael busied himself with arranging my legs, parting them just enough so he could guide his thick cock into my dripping folds.

I gasped, pushing back with the help of the guiding hands he placed on my hips. He sank every thick, beautiful inch of himself into me, the angle making him press deliciously against that one spot that made sparkles somewhere right underneath my heart.

Still, it wasn't enough. I leaned up enough to almost reach Rudy's ear. "Turn over so I can suck you."

Rudy was awake. He nimbly twisted out from under my arm, scooting up on the bed.

Michael pushed me to my knees without ever losing his place inside me.

I ended up exactly where I wanted to be, with my face right above Rudy's long, steel-hard cock. Wrapping my arms around Rudy's thighs, I took him into my mouth as Michael commenced to pounding behind me. My sweatpants and Michael's thighs kept my legs together, making me that much tighter for him. There was no way in hell I was getting all of Rudy into my mouth, but I'd found that paying special attention to the tip of his cock was plenty for him.

Rudy threaded his fingers into my hair, gently guiding me. He murmured encouragement, his voice sunk to the chocolate depths it only reached during sex.

Since I was already squirming from the exquisite feel of Michael's thick cock abrading my inner walls, I just tried to concentrate on sucking. Accidentally my teeth scraped the firm ridge of the head of Rudy's cock, and his entire body bucked. I glanced up at him, worried I'd hurt him, prepared to apologize, but his head was thrown back and the look on his face—as much as I could see—was full of anything but pain. His mouth dropped open, a moan of pure pleasure spilling from his lips. I tried it again, gently, and he bucked again, head thrashing side to side.

Brutally strong violet passion poured into me through Rudy's leash, so amazing that I very nearly came. I tamped it down, wanting this to last. Screwing my eyes shut, I sucked hard, moaning. I caught his pleasure, mixed it with my own, and gathered Michael's mounting crimson burn. The combination of the three made a heady concoction that made it confusing to know who was who and who was doing what. But it didn't matter. We were all there. We were all one.

We all came hard in an explosion of all of the colors of power.

I lay with my cheek against Rudy's belly, able to hear his heavy breathing through his abdomen. I was blissfully out of breath myself. Michael matched us from where he lay sprawled half on top of me. It was lovely. I could have stayed there all day.

No, I couldn't!

My head snapped up, barely missing smacking Michael's nose. "What time is it?"

"Hey!" he groused, flopping onto his back and away from my flailing limbs.

I scrambled up, careful not to maul Rudy, and crawled off the bed. Neither Rudy nor Michael believed in alarm clocks, so there was no red or blue LED face glowing at me to show the time. I actually had to pad across the hall to find my cell phone, fighting with my T-shirt and sweats along the way. I hadn't a clue where my socks had gone.

It was only nine o'clock. Good. I still had time. I was supposed to be at the store already, but I wasn't too late. I flipped open the phone and dialed the shop.

"Wow, you called."

I ignored Gwen's flippant tone. "Yeah. Sorry. I just got up." I pulled clothes out of my bag. "I'm jumping in the shower now. I should be there before ten."

"Really?"

I sighed. "Really."

"Okay."

"See ya soon. Bye."

As I flipped the phone closed, a thrill of apprehension ran through me. Was Michael going to fight me?

Arms full of clothing, I stomped back into the bedroom. The bathroom off the master bedroom had, by far, the best shower. I sensed Rudy in the bathroom, somewhere behind the mostly closed door.

Michael lay on his back on the bed, forearm slung over his eyes. He looked so very yummy all sweaty and mussed, it was a shame I couldn't climb on top of him. He must have felt me staring. He turned his head on the pillow, cracking his eyes open halfway under the cover of his arm.

We shared a long, silent stare before I had to know. "Are we going to fight about this?"

"About your putting yourself in danger?"

I scowled.

"It's a bad idea."

"Michael…"

"We'll be with her." I turned to see Rudy standing in the bathroom door, eyes on Michael as he dried his hands with a green and white striped towel. "Even if she loses control, we can figure something out."

I glanced at Michael, who scowled at Rudy. "Still too dangerous. Besides, I have to go to the courthouse for at least a little while today."

Rudy shrugged, twisting a bit so he could toss the towel behind him onto the unseen counter. "So I'll be with her."

I looked back in time to see it in Michael's eyes. I knew he trusted Rudy. He'd loved Rudy long before I came into the picture. But it was clear that he didn't trust Rudy *quite* enough for this.

Rudy stepped up to the bed, slinging an arm around my shoulders. I could tell by the look in his eyes that he knew it, too. But he was so much more easygoing than me. Either that, or he was more used to working Michael. He kept his cool and cocked his head to the side, grinning. "C'mon, Mike, she was fine yesterday. And even the day before wasn't so bad."

"With no one else around."

"I can handle it," I blurted.

He glanced at me.

Rudy squeezed my shoulder. "We'll never know until we try."

"It's too soon." I opened my mouth to protest, but Michael sat up, continuing to talk. "But I can see that no matter what I say, neither one of you is going to listen." He scooted to the far edge of the bed, putting his back to us. "I'll drive you to the shop. I can stay about an hour. I'll go to the courthouse and be back within a few hours." He stood and turned to us, one raven brow arched. "Do you think the two of you can stay out of trouble that long?"

I bit my lip over a retort. I'd won. Sometimes I know when to keep my mouth shut. I met his gaze quite seriously. "Thank you."

He was surprised. I could see it even if it didn't show much. He blinked and gave me a very small grin before turning his head back and closing his eyes again. "Go take a shower. And be quick. We all need one."

I snorted, turning toward the bathroom. "Who decided that we needed a wake-up fuck?"

"Complaining?"

I grinned as I nudged the bathroom door mostly closed. "Nope."

Chapter Four

We were about halfway through the thirty-minute drive when I thought to ask. "What do you have to go to court for?"

Michael glanced at me briefly before turning his eyes back to the road. He looked so crisp and official with his hair pulled back into a ponytail and in his pressed, button-down shirt with the tiny blue pinstripes. He even had a blue and violet tie looped loosely about his collar. The early morning sun barely broke through the gloomy fog, but it was enough to make him cover those marvelous green eyes with sunglasses. They looked like cop glasses except that they weren't mirrored, so I could see his eyes. I'd bet they were a lot more expensive than cop glasses, too. "Cook wants me to meet some people." I waited, but no more was forthcoming.

I knew Cook was Howard Cook, the district attorney. Cook was human and, as far as I knew, not a witch, but he was deep enough in the government that he knew about shifters. Both Cook and Michael were part of the large coalition that worked diligently to keep the vast majority of the human race from realizing that witches and shifters really existed. Cook worked through Legal Affairs with a select few in the know who were scattered among his employ. He also worked with private detectives like Michael, both shifters and non-shifters, who supplied information for men like Cook. It was a delicate balance, especially in the last forty years or so as mass media became more and more prevalent. Back in the middle ages or even in the 1700s, keeping the secret had been easier. Now, there was a huge organization of shifters and witches whose sole purpose in life was to keep our secret. They infiltrated the media and the government, making sure stories got squashed and evidence went missing. Some stories they'd let through, either in gossip rags or as sitcoms or those supposed reality shows. As long as no one got *too* close to the truth and couldn't prove anything, they usually let it slide. They also served to police witches and shifters, enforcing the laws of the Witches' Council.

"Anyone in particular he wants you to meet?"

"I doubt you'd know them."

"You're probably right, but entertain me."

He threw me a sidelong glance.

I smiled brightly at him, showing teeth.

If I'm any judge, he barely managed to not roll his eyes as he turned them back to the road. "Cook and the police chief are deciding whether to keep me as an investigator or to make me an enforcer. Seems LA needs more muscle in special operations. They want me to meet more of the local shifters in charge before deciding."

I frowned. "Being an enforcer is dangerous."

The corner of his lip twitched up slightly. "Yes."

Enforcers were like the shifter and witch police. They were the ones who tracked down rogue shifters or went and took down witches with delusions of grandeur. I didn't want him to be an enforcer, but neither did I want to dictate his life. I was well aware that the pendulum swung both ways. "Is that what you want to do?"

"Not especially, but I was considering it."

I glanced in the back seat at Rudy, who stared out the window. He felt me looking at him and glanced at me. I couldn't see his eyes behind black Ray-Bans, but he smiled and shrugged.

I turned back to Michael. "Was? You've changed your mind?"

Now Michael did smile, although he stayed facing front. "Don't you know? They don't like to make leashed shifters enforcers."

It never occurred to me before. I'd known about enforcers my whole life, of course, but it hadn't dawned on me that none of them were leashed. Of course, all the leashed shifters I'd known belonged to witches in powerful places. Witches who needed and could afford to have personal bodyguards.

He shrugged. "Obviously, my situation has changed since I last met with them."

I stared at his profile. "Did I ruin your chances at something you wanted to do?"

He glanced at me. His smile looked warm. "No. I'm perfectly happy being an investigator."

"It's what he's good at, anyway." Rudy leaned forward to briefly squeeze Michael's shoulder. "Not that he wouldn't make a kick-ass enforcer."

Michael glanced at him in the rearview mirror. "Flattery will get you everywhere."

I smiled and sat back in my seat. For the moment, at least, we were back on solid ground. I decided to be a good girl and not provoke a fight.

We reached the parking lot down the block from the outdoor shopping mall that surrounded my store. We actually parked next to my blue PT Cruiser. Rudy spent a few minutes making me open it so he could see inside, proclaiming that he loved the style of the car. I indulged him, noting as I did that Michael stood back and kept his eyes on our surroundings.

I finally dragged Rudy out of my car and walked hand-in-hand with him toward the open cross-section to the pedestrian walk for the mall. Michael stayed slightly behind us, and when I glanced back, he was still checking out the buildings and the few people around us. Of course, so was Rudy. He was a bit more circumspect, but I noticed him glancing over my head briefly before he met my eyes.

Bodyguards, lovers, and, I hoped, eventually close friends, but for the moment they were first and foremost bodyguards. Their lives were quite literally tied to mine by the magic leashes. They could survive my death, but not unless I thought to release the leashes first, or without help from another witch.

We made it to my little bookstore and internet café and walked through the glass door in front, making the cheery overhead bell ring. Off to the left were the rows of bookshelves and paperback racks. To the right were four rows of computer cubbies, six cubbies to each row. In each cubby was a computer, rentable by the hour. It was there that our business really made its money. Although we did have some mundane customers, most of our clientele were witches. They found out about me through the grapevine and knew I could lead them to all sorts of information. There were programs and internet links I knew of that were a source of great comfort and help to many witches.

It was funny, really. I'd come across most of the links and tidbits of information because I was a horrible student. My long-term memory for spells and history was abysmal. I was okay in the short term, but usually once I no longer had use for a spell, it went out of my head. So I'd started keeping notes. A child of the twenty-first century, I'd kept those notes on computer. I'd also gathered links and contact information for quite a few sources for various bits of information all over the world. Those little bits of knowledge now supported me. Strange how the world worked, sometimes.

Gwen was leaning over the counter, elbows braced on a short stack of books, talking to one of our regular customers. Greg was a balding man in his early thirties who almost exactly matched my five-foot-ten height. He was the pastor of a local church and a closet witch. He often came to the shop, looking for justification of his faith. I liked him despite his stubborn determination that the Goddess was a God.

They both looked up at our entrance, and Greg's eyes went wide at the sight of the tall men flanking me. He might not have looked twice at Rudy, dressed in his preferred worn jeans and T-shirt, with his denim jacket dangling over his back from the two fingers he rested on his shoulder. But Michael in his court wear, with his jacket draped over a forearm and his wrist banded by an expensive Rolex, made him look twice.

"Morning, Greg," I greeted, trying to act normal.

"Meg!" He stepped forward, arms out for a hug. A low, barely heard growl from behind my right shoulder stopped him.

Without looking, I flung a backhand, hitting Michael square in the chest. "Quit it. Greg's a friend of mine."

I heard his sniff and ignored it, stepping into Greg's aborted embrace. He hugged me, but I saw his worried eyes on Michael when I pulled back.

"Didn't Gwen tell you?"

Greg dragged his eyes from Michael, glanced at Rudy, then looked at me. No doubt the height of my shifters put him on edge as well. "She told me you'd leashed two shifters but..." He laughed nervously. "I guess it hadn't sunk in."

"You're not alone," I heard Michael mutter.

I glared at him, but he missed it, too busy walking down the far aisle of the bookshelves, glancing down each row.

"So." I turned back to Greg, putting on a smile. "What are you buying today?"

He walked with me back to the counter. "Oh, nothing important. Gwen was showing me the new Jim Butcher book, though."

"Jim Butcher!" Rudy appeared at his other side, making Greg jump. "I *love* his books!" He leaned back against the counter, elbows braced on the metal edge. "Which one are you getting?"

Bless his heart. Rudy's enthusiasm soon had Greg in an animated discussion, diffusing the tension.

I listened to them talk, keeping an eye on Michael. He finished walking the bookshelves, then inspected the computer cubbies. He left no doubt that he was casing the place, making sure he knew the layout. I couldn't decide if I was flattered or annoyed.

Gwen's hand on my arm distracted me. I looked down into big blue eyes, framed by a doll's face. The fact that she wore her long blonde hair in two ponytails that flounced over her shoulders and down her back only added to the effect. To top it off, she often—like today—dressed like a schoolgirl. Or the popular version of a schoolgirl, anyway. She wore a plaid blue and white skirt and a blue sweater with matching opaque tights. She even wore heeled Mary Janes on her feet. Worry, relief, and unfortunately anger battled in her gaze. "You came."

"I said I would."

She nodded, searching my face. Not sure what for, but she didn't seem to find it. "Yeah, you did."

I smiled and pulled her into a hug. The top of her head fit neatly under my chin. "I'm sorry I bailed on you."

She clutched me shamelessly. "Are you okay?" she asked into my shoulder.

"Yeah. I'm good."

"I was so scared."

Understandable. The last time she'd seen me, Roland Parks had taken me to his house to claim ownership. I'd called her the next morning to make sure she knew I was okay, but in these situations there was nothing like verifying a person's existence with your own two eyes.

"I know." I looked over her head to see Rudy and Greg watching us. "Rudy, can you watch things out here for a while?"

He cocked his head to the side, frowning at me from beneath heavy bangs that pretty much hid his eyes. "I don't know how to work the register or anything."

"It's okay. Just be here. Call us if someone else comes in." I looked at Greg. "That okay?"

Greg waved his hand in the air. "Absolutely. I'll start up one of the computers in a bit, if you don't mind."

"Nope. Help yourself." I looked at Rudy. "Greg's already got a pass code, so he doesn't need any help."

Gwen pulled from my hug and turned to the doorless entry that led to the back of the shop. She kept her head down and averted, clearly hiding tears. A hand on her back, I followed her.

Michael trailed us. When I looked up at him, he nodded toward the back exit. "I'll sit back here." He held up a paperback he must have picked up from one of the racks. "Mind if I read this?"

He was being so nice. I knew he didn't want to be here—didn't want *us* to be here—but he was making the best of it. I reached out and squeezed his arm. "There's a ratty chair in that room." I pointed toward the storeroom just off the back door. "It looks horrible, but it's clean and comfortable."

He nodded, then stuck his head into the office to look around. After that brief look, he went into the storeroom, closing the office door behind him.

Gwen was perched on the edge of the desk, looking more like a high-schooler than a twenty-two-year-old woman. She carefully wiped at tears with her fingertips, trying not to smudge the heavy black mascara she wore. "I'm surprised he let you come."

I hovered near the grungy barred window opposite the desk. "He almost didn't."

"Why?"

"He says it's dangerous."

She glanced at the closed door. "Can he hear us?"

"I don't think so. Not unless we talk loud. Rudy's the one with the really good hearing."

She nodded, returning her gaze to her knees. "Right. Wolf."

"Yep."

She swung her feet a little. "Why's it dangerous? Roland's gone, right?"

"Yeah, he is."

She cocked her head so one eye could look at me. "That's a good thing."

I sighed. "Yeah."

Her head came up, ponytails whipping behind her as she sat straight and glowered at me. "Meg, don't you *dare* tell me that you're sorry he's dead!"

I scratched at chipped paint on the barred window. "I didn't want him dead, Gwen. I just wanted him gone from my life."

"Damn it, Meg, that bastard would have completely taken over your life. I know damn well you didn't even tell me all the things he wanted to do to you. He deserves whatever he got."

The memory of his shocked face as I drained him of life and power flashed across my mind. I raised a hand to press thumb and forefinger into my eyes as though that could banish the sight. "Sure."

"Meg."

I dropped my hand, blinked, then raised my head to look at her. "What?"

I couldn't decide if she was worried or angry. Her eyes were narrowed, brows beetled over them, but her mouth was twisted in concern. Maybe she couldn't decide either. "What's wrong? Why is it dangerous for you to be here? Are his people after you?"

I shook my head, wiping a hand across my face. "We don't think so."

"Meg, *talk* to me."

I opened my mouth, paused, then shut it. I shook my head. "I...can't, Gwen. There's stuff going on that if you knew..."

She sniffed. "What? I'm not a strong enough witch to help you?"

"That's not it."

"It usually is."

"No, Gwen, it's not. Please, let's not do this."

"Do what? I can't possibly do anything because I don't know what's *going on!*"

"And you're safer that way." I walked around behind the desk, avoiding her simmering concern. "Where are the papers for this month?"

"Meg…" Her back was to me, her head tilted so that she was probably staring at our Luis Royo print that hung on the opposite wall by the window.

I shuffled through some open bills that sat on the desktop, not really seeing them as I sat. "This is what I needed to come in for, isn't it? First of the month and all."

She sat silent. I couldn't see her face, but I felt red anger rolling off of her. Eventually, she hopped down and turned. Her face was studiously bland and she wouldn't meet my eyes. "Everything's here." She leaned forward and rearranged papers and bills in front of me as I sat. "I just kept the stack like you usually do. I entered some of the information into QuickBooks, but you'll probably need to check it. I couldn't manage to send any of the online bill payments."

I nodded, jiggling the mouse to wake up the computer.

"I'll be out front if you need me." Gwen left.

Not two minutes later, Michael came in. I only glanced at him as he sauntered over to the old couch underneath the window. He sat, and another glance told me that he really was reading the paperback that he'd picked up.

I bit my lip to hold back tears that suddenly wanted to well up. He was protecting me and trying not to make a major thing of it. It made me want to go over there and sink into his arms. But I was the one who'd made a big deal about coming in to take care of the shop, so I needed to take care of the shop.

About an hour later, Michael stood and came to the desk. I looked up just as he reached out to cup my chin.

He smiled softly. "I've got to go."

I nodded.

He looked so nice. But I did miss the errant lock that usually tried to hide his right eye. It had been moussed into submission, plastered back on his head.

He leaned down to kiss me, a brief, soft meeting of lips. "You be good." As he straightened, he pushed my cell phone across the desktop, closer to my side. "Call me if something happens."

I nodded and watched his fine ass walk out the door. I'd be lying to say that a small tendril of dread didn't go through me at his departure. Through the last week, Michael had been a rock, and I'm quite sure I'd be Roland's plaything now if it weren't for the shapeshifter. Too bad he was so damn bossy!

Minutes later, Rudy appeared in the doorway, thumbs hooked in the threadbare waist of his jeans. He grinned at me from underneath his shaggy mane of hair. "Hey. You okay?"

"I'm fine."

His gaze shifted around the room, taking it in. He backed up a step to glance down the hall to the back door. "That door locked?"

I had to smile. "It should be. Michael checked it."

He laughed. "Okay, okay. Just making sure. He made me swear I'd look out for you, and he's a big guy and all." He snorted as he stepped into the room and up to the desk. "Like I would let anything happen to you." He leaned on the far edge of the desk, and I couldn't help but admire the bunch of muscles shown off by the tight fit of his T-shirt. "You want me to stay in here with you?"

I shook my head, turning back to the computer screen. "You don't have to."

"Do you want me to?"

I let a small smile curl my lips. "No. You'd just distract me."

"Oh?" Although he was a canine, he did a pretty nifty purr sometimes. "I distract you?"

I looked in time to see him purposely flex his arms. I laughed. "You know you do, you sexy devil."

He shook his head, grinning. "Sexy *beast*, Meg. When will you get that right?"

"You'll just have to keep coaching me."

"Mmmm." He leaned farther over the desk, closer to me. "I guess so." He cocked his head to the side, every inch the irresistible young man I was fast losing my heart to. If I hadn't already. "Kiss?"

Gladly, I leaned up and pressed my mouth to his. Cheeky beast that he was, he swiped his tongue over my lips, parting them so he could taste my mouth.

When we parted, he gazed at me with dreamy, crystal-blue eyes. His voice was husky when he asked, "Want me to stay in here with you?"

I smiled and shook my head. "Not necessary. Unless you're sick of being out front."

He stood. "Actually, it's kind of fun. Gwen's teaching me how to ring up sales."

I rolled my eyes. "Oh, Goddess. Now we are in trouble."

He scrunched his nose and stuck his tongue out at me.

"Careful where you stick that. I might make you use it."

"Promises, promises." He turned, waving. "Yell if you need me. I'm leaving this door open."

"I think I'll always need you," I murmured, turning back to the computer.

"I heard that," he said softly, just as he disappeared.

Chapter Five

It was an hour before closing and I was reviewing the books. I'd stayed in the office like a good little girl, taking only bathroom breaks. I'd even eaten lunch in the office. If Michael conceded to my need to come to the shop, I decided that I didn't have to make matters worse by being "in public" more than necessary. Rudy came in regularly to check on me, and we were doing just fine.

Michael called to let us know he'd been delayed. His meetings had proven to draw more people than were originally intended. Against his better judgment, we agreed that Rudy and I would drive back to their place in my car after we closed shop for the day.

Everything seemed to be in order. Bills were paid for October, and November payments were scheduled. I even managed to get to some other stuff finished that I'd put off before Halloween. I was almost ahead of the game. Shocking.

I was just turning to the computer to start browsing the internet for Thanksgiving decorating ideas when Gwen appeared in the doorway. I looked up, and my smile died when I saw her wide-eyed look. "What?"

"You should probably come out here."

I was on my feet and headed toward her in an instant. "What's wrong?"

Reaching the entry to the front of the shop, I saw before she could answer.

Rudy stood in the opening of the counter, arms braced on either side to prevent anyone from passing by him toward the back of the shop. Standing before him was a tiny, slim blonde woman with huge brown eyes. She kind of looked like that singer Jewel, complete with the fragile look. That she wore a fluffy, cream angora sweater and—I kid you not—pink slacks added to the softly feminine look. She hugged a pink clutch purse to her breast, obviously intimidated by my wolf. The moment I appeared, she turned to me and the shattered desperation that shot at me through those big eyes struck me like a tidal wave.

Then I recognized her. But not from any personal experience. Oh, no. I remembered her, but what I remembered was her soft, naked body writhing underneath me while I pounded my cock into the velvet vise of her pussy. I remembered holding her down and ignoring her cries of pain because she wasn't quite ready for me. I remembered not caring. I remembered liking her pain. I remembered shattering her spirit, then capturing her magic and forcing her to submit to my will, body and soul.

Her name was Chloe; the recollections were not mine, but Roland Parks's.

Shit!

Only shock kept me from blurting her name. I clamped down on it and the roil of power that surged with Roland's thoughts. Stepping forward, I laid my hand on the small of Rudy's back. Touching him helped to calm the confusion to a manageable level. For the moment. Hoping it wasn't too obvious, I slid my hand up under the untucked hem of his shirt, seeking the warm skin of his lower back.

"Please," Chloe's soft voice entreated as she stepped toward me. She stopped at Rudy's ominous growl, but kept her focus on me. One small, ringed hand reached for me. "Please, you've got to help us."

By sheer force of will, I gathered my strength and spoke to her. "Do I know you?" It was a miracle my voice came out normal and calm. I hoped my face matched it.

She blinked, and the hand reaching for me hovered back toward her. "I...I thought you might." She frowned, and it looked out of place on her sunny face. "I'm Chloe. Chloe Vance. I...I was with...I mean, I was at Roland's house on...Samhain."

I let her stutter, not wanting to show that I knew exactly who she was. That I knew more about her than she realized. She wasn't a very powerful or sensitive witch. A sporadic psychic and moderately useful conduit. It had not been a great feat for Roland to take her. She'd given herself willingly enough at first, and once he'd made inroads, taking over her life had been a pleasure for him.

The bastard!

"I'm sorry." I dug my fingers into Rudy's flesh, desperately trying to keep the rush of memories under wraps. "I didn't really get a chance to meet everyone that night."

Her face fell and she stepped back. Her hovering hand landed on the upper swell of her left breast. "No. I don't suppose you did." Anxiously, she studied my face. "Are you...all right?"

I shrugged. "As all right as I can be."

"Oh. That's...good."

Her stuttering speech started to get on my nerves. My stolen memories recalled that she did that a lot. Roland had liked it a heck of a lot more than I did.

"I take it you were part of his *coven?*" I let every bit of my disdain drip through the word, because it hadn't been a coven. It'd been more of a slave ring. And he'd wanted me as the top slave.

Again I say, the bastard!

She flinched, gaze dropping to the floor. "Yes. I...we...He'd intended for you to join us later that night."

In a flash, I remembered the gist of the conversation. He'd told them what he was going to do. They knew almost as much about me as Roland had. He'd compared every one of them to me and found them lacking. He'd crowed that I was coming to rule them.

Of course, I'd messed up his plans and killed him. Shame on me. The women were featured in a bunch of area newspapers November first, each of them listed as living in his house. Roland had set himself up as a regular Hugh

Hefner. Okay, maybe not as many girls as Hugh, but having five women living with him without being married to any of them had done wonders for his reputation.

"Yeah, well. I wasn't up for that."

She raised those doe eyes to me again, glancing briefly at Rudy. I couldn't see his face, but there was no mistaking his defensive posture. She wasn't getting near me.

"I know," she said, turning back to me. Desperation was back. "That's why…that's why I'm here. Please, you've got to help us."

"Help who?"

"Us. Our…coven." Oh, yeah, she'd heard my disdain. She wasn't stupid, just terribly naïve and shy.

"What does the coven have to do with me?"

"We're still connected."

"So?"

She blinked at me. "You don't feel it?"

I frowned. I felt a lot of things. "Feel what?"

Her jaw dropped, glossed pink lips shining around a small, darker pink mouth. "You…us…we're linked."

"Come again?"

"Could you be that powerful? Can't you feel the link? We can."

"What?"

She nodded. "You're connected to us."

"How? I didn't join your coven." Did I? My exact memories of Halloween and the time I was trapped in Roland's power circle were hazy. I'd been concentrating on getting my magic back. Then when I had, my anger had erupted. Once the big magics started flowing, it had been all I could do to keep my sanity.

She shook her head. "None of us know enough about it to know how it happened. As you probably already know, Roland didn't...tell us much."

"So how do you know we're connected?" Inwardly, I poked through what I knew of that night, both as me and as Roland, trying to delve underneath them to find this connection she was talking about. But it was all such a jumble, I was having trouble keeping my thoughts from merging too closely with Roland's memories.

"We thought the link would just fade away without Roland. After all, none of us know how to keep it together. We thought the connection we felt might just be residual from Halloween night. We've stayed in the house. The enforcers and Roland's business associates have been very nice about it—"

Would she ever get to the point?

"—but, it's been almost a week and we're still...*connected*." She searched my face. "There's something that Roland did to us that's still there. It's connected to you. How can you not feel it?"

I had a real bad feeling about this.

She bit her lip, wringing her hands together. "We thought his death would free us. But...it hasn't."

I frowned. "You've all done magic together. Why wouldn't you stay connected?"

She shook her head. "We haven't."

"What?"

"Roland never worked magic with us. He worked through us."

As she spoke, his memories surfaced and I saw something I hadn't seen before. I'd known something was wrong with his magic that I hadn't been able to put my finger on. A coven's magic was supposed to be shared. Yes, one person might lead the spell, but the others were supposed to be an active part of it. Roland hadn't done that. Instead, he'd drained their magic, incorporating it into his own. His spells were solitary. Now it made sense that the women hadn't been in the circle that night. He'd kept them apart. They were like batteries or generators. They were connected to him and fed him energy, but they were mindless pieces of his power.

I lowered my gaze, staring at my sneakers. Good Goddess! By draining him, had I taken on his coven, too? This *so* sucked!

"You do understand," I heard her say.

"Not really."

"But, you're a witch…"

I glared at her through my bangs. "And if Roland told you anything at all about me, he should have mentioned that I'm not a very good one."

Rudy shot me a look over his shoulder, but I ignored it. Michael didn't want me saying such things to other people, but I'd been doing it for so long, it was habit.

Chloe's confusion was evident. Then her face cleared into a look of horror. "That's why he wanted you. So powerful, but without training."

"Bingo."

She glanced at Rudy. "But you have protection." Was that envy in her voice? If so, I don't think it was just because Rudy was so damn cute.

"Desperate times called for desperate measures."

"Hey," Rudy protested.

I pinched him lightly and almost smiled.

She rushed forward, reaching. I stumbled back, right into Gwen. Rudy caught Chloe before she got to me, holding her back. It was only then that I realized we were the only four in the shop, thank the Goddess.

"Please!" Chloe reached toward me over the arm Rudy had banded around her middle. "Please, you have to help us."

I scowled, stepping away from Gwen. "I'll try and figure out how to dissolve the coven, okay? I don't want it any more than you do."

"No, that's not it. You can't just dissolve it!"

Now she was pissing me off. "Then what the hell do you want?"

She cringed and I almost felt bad. Almost. "You have to come out to the house."

"Roland's house?"

"Yes."

"Not a chance."

"Please! There's a will. He left everything to us. To his coven. If you dissolve it…"

"So this is about *money?*"

Rudy set her down and released her, stepping back toward me. He pulled out his cell phone out and flipped it open. I hoped he was calling Michael.

Chloe wrung her hands together. "Please, you've got to understand."

"Stop saying 'please'!"

Chloe again clutched her bag to her chest. "Just come out to the house. Talk to us. We need to find a way to work this out. Please. Roland's lawyer, Thomas, is there tonight. He can tell us what we can do."

On some level, I was relieved that this was about money and not about power. That made it all much more mundane and easier to manage somehow.

I sank against the wall. Without touching Rudy, it was harder to fight the memories. I had to focus hard to speak normally. "I'll think about it."

Gwen stepped in front of me, placing her small body between the little woman and me. Instinct told me to touch Gwen, but I didn't, afraid the memories would spill into her somehow.

"But you must come. Tonight."

"There's no *must* about this! I don't want anything to do with you."

My tone worked like a slap, and only then did I realize that it was the exact tone Roland had used when he expected to be obeyed. I hoped that her obedience was just an instinct thing and that she didn't find it familiar. She took another step backwards, toward the shop's main door, hugging that clutch purse hard to her chest as she bowed her head. "I'm sorry."

I closed my eyes, thumping my head against the wall at my back. "Look, why don't you go home. Give me a phone number. I'll call you when—"

"You killed him," she whispered, voice barely audible. "You drained his magic and left him an empty husk."

I stilled. I was very glad that there were no customers around. Unfortunately, Gwen was and I heard her gasp. Rudy flipped his phone closed and stepped back, headed my way.

I had to say something. "It was self-defense." No use hiding it. Michael and I had discussed it. The enforcers would know I'd killed him. Self-defense was permissible and justifiable in that situation.

Her eyes lifted, steady now, desperation making them so. "At first, yes. But we felt it. You could have stopped. You should have stopped. You *drained* him. You ripped his mind to shreds. What else did you get from him?"

Rudy growled, tensed to lunge at her.

Desperate, I reached around Gwen and caught his T-shirt, dragging him back toward me. I needed his touch more than I needed him going after Chloe Vance.

Eyes rounded, Chloe stepped back. "If we go to the grand dame, we'd have to tell her that."

The grand dame of the Southwest United States. Shannon Cavanagh. A childhood nemesis of mine. Exactly the person I *didn't* want to become involved in this.

I didn't care if it looked like I was hiding. I stepped into Rudy's back. He turned and put his arms around me, pressing my shoulder into his chest, my hip into his groin.

I glared at the woman. "You're blackmailing me?"

Tears spilled down her cheeks. "I don't want to. But we need your help."

"What do you want? Exactly?"

"You have to come to the house. We have to decide together what to do about the coven."

"What's kept you from going to Shannon already?"

"She'll break the coven."

"And you won't get your inheritance."

She said nothing. She didn't have to.

"This bites." My anger and Rudy's touch just managed to keep the storm at bay.

"Just come to the house. Please. W-we can work this out."

"Can we?"

"Please." Her favorite word.

I stared down at the counter at the price sheet for renting the shop's computers for internet use. "I'll have to think about it."

"You can't…"

I glared up at her, making her fall back another step. "You can't expect me to just come out to that house, can you? Do you realize I almost died there?"

"Yes, but we need—"

"You need to give me some time to think about it."

Her mouth fell open. "You have to come. Now."

I frowned at her. "Why?"

"Everyone's...I mean, we need..."

I cocked my head to the side. "I don't like that house. I never intended to go back. I need some time to gear up for it, okay? Leave me a number to call you."

"But..."

"But what? You were supposed to get me out there tonight? Throwing a little party for me?"

She backed up a step. "N-no. Nothing like that. It's just that Thomas will be there tonight..."

"Thomas can come back."

"But we could call Shannon—"

"Look, do you want my help or not? If not, then call Shannon up right now." It was a gamble, but she was pissing me off and I needed to get her out of there. I had to sort these memories out of my head and deal with the surging power pressing underneath my diaphragm.

She blinked. "No, please, I—"

"I'm done discussing this." I turned in Rudy's embrace, aiming myself for the office. "Leave a number and I'll call you."

"But..."

I turned at the entrance to the back, holding Rudy's hands in a death grip that I hoped Chloe couldn't see. "I don't want anything to do with all this, but it looks like I don't have a choice. I'll do what I can to help get all of us out of this without you losing your inheritance."

"It's yours as well."

I shook my head. "I don't want anything of Roland's." I already had enough, thank you.

"But…it's millions…"

"Yeah. And you guys are welcome to it." I was shaking, starting to lose my grip on my anger and, therefore, the power and memories. I had to get away from her. "Leave your number and I'll call you tomorrow. You've got my word on it."

I pulled Rudy after me into the office. Gwen was right on our heels.

Rudy sat me on the couch but remained standing. His hand stayed on my neck as I slumped forward over my knees. "Let me go make sure she's gone. You'll be okay for a minute?"

Would I? "Hurry," I told him, hugging my thighs.

Gwen dropped to her knees before me. I felt her rubbing my back in large, soothing circles. "Meg, what's happening?"

I swallowed, screwing my eyes shut in vain against the visions that were never witnessed by my own eyes. "Not now, Gwen. Go away."

"Meg, tell me what's wrong. What can I do to help?"

I shook my head and heard the odd keening that started in the back of my throat. Roland's memories were surging, telling me way more about his coven and about Chloe Vance than I ever wanted to know. So much that I couldn't process it. But neither could I let it go. It was like a tornado trying to fill a china ball. The ball just wasn't going to hold it. Unfortunately, I was the ball.

"Meg!" Gwen's voice sounded far away.

Rudy was back. He peeled my arms from around my thighs and hauled me to my feet. My inarticulate whine continued even as his arms gathered around me, knocking the tornado briefly aside.

I burrowed into him, able to think for a moment, but the storm remained, battering at my very brief control.

"You should go watch the front," Rudy told Gwen, his tone brooking no argument as he cradled my head in the bend of his neck. His other hand untucked my shirt, sliding underneath to give me skin-to-skin.

"What? What do you mean? What's happening?"

The hand at the back of my skull gathered in my hair and used it to pull my head back. I gasped, not expecting it. Rudy took advantage of my parted lips to kiss me, swiping his tongue quickly inside. The touch of his lips and the taste of his tongue were brief, but they broke the storm enough that the keening in my throat stopped.

"Gwen, leave!" Rudy spoke with his lips on my forehead. "We've gotta take care of this."

"Take care of what?"

"Gwen, please," I rasped.

"What the *hell* is going on?! You're not planning on doing what I think you are."

Frustration. Fear. Something of both. I did *not* want Gwen to know or see any of this. That wish stirred the power that burbled just along the surface of my soul. I flung my hand toward her, fingers splayed out, and used the power to push her toward the door. I didn't see her reaction. I didn't have time to care. I turned and grabbed Rudy's head, angling his lips for a hard, punishing kiss. My thigh came up so that I could wrap my ankle around his knee. He was my only haven in the maelstrom, and I clung for dear life.

He knew what I needed, and bless him, he was ready for it. He let me cling to him like a baby monkey as he fumbled at my jeans. I dropped my leg for him and my arms as well so I could tug at his shirt. I whimpered, determined to focus on him and not on the vague recollections that wanted to crowd my mind. The physicality of him, of us, was what helped. It was what allowed me to push Roland aside.

He got my jeans down, and I toed out of my shoes while he unbuttoned his fly. He fell back onto the couch, pushing his jeans only halfway down his thighs, enough to expose that wonderfully hard, red cock of his. Barely waiting for me to step out of my own jeans, he yanked me down to straddle his lap. The rough, bunched denim of his jeans scratched the sensitive inside of my legs, to be replaced by the hot, slightly hairy skin of his thighs as I scrambled into position. As soon as I could, I slammed my dripping pussy down on his cock, breaking our kiss so we could both gasp as the sudden, painful pleasure. Rudy was actually a bit too long for me, so there really was pain as he butted up to my cervix, but the pain actually helped. It rooted me in myself. In what we were doing. I rode him for all I was worth, keening now for an entirely different reason. Somewhere before we came, the tornado of memories died, dissolving in the waves of heat that crashed over us as we both strove for climax.

I sat in his lap, sated. Myself again. His arms surrounded me, one hand rubbing my back gently and the other cupping the back of my skull, tucking my head under his chin. I listened to his heartbeat slow down again, matched my calming breath to his. Tears I hadn't been aware of shedding dampened the collar of his T-shirt.

"Fuck," I finally said.

He laughed, more exasperation than mirth. "Yeah."

"Michael's gonna be pissed."

"We couldn't have called that one, Meg." He ran soothing hands over my back. "You were doing fine until she showed up."

Glum, I pushed back from his embrace. I stayed straddling his lap, my hands braced on his shoulders. His cock softened gradually, slipping out of me. "Maybe I should have called it. It's scary that they're linked to me and I didn't know it."

He shrugged, unable to argue the point.

I shook my head, tears still streaming down my face. "I don't want to do this anymore, Rudy."

He said nothing, just gathered me back into his embrace and let me cry.

I took the comfort, gladly.

Gwen was a pillar of ice, albeit a short one, when we finally put ourselves back together and re-emerged. The closed sign hung from the door and she was turning off the computers. Gray-lavender twilight tinged by the dirty gold of the awakening lamps outside lit the room. It was too early to close shop, but I wasn't going to argue with her.

"Gwen, we've...uh, got to go."

She refused to look up at me. "Yeah, I figured."

"I'm sorry."

"For what?"

I blinked at her. I hated that calm, cold tone. It meant she was tamping down her emotions, which meant that they were really strong.

"You didn't need to see that." I gestured vaguely toward the back of the shop.

"No. Of course not." Briskly, she straightened and finally faced me. I couldn't decipher the look on her face. Anger? Horror? Concern? All of the above? Yeah, all of those, with a healthy dose of resentment. None of the emotions I wanted to see in my best friend. "Not any of my business."

"Gwen..."

She shrugged, turning toward the desk and crossing her arms over her chest. "Nothing you've been going through is any of my business...obviously. I didn't know half of the things you were talking about just then. I was in the way."

Shit!

"But that's okay. You don't want me to know."

"Gwen, that's not it. There just hasn't been any time—"

The anger won out. Her light gold eyebrows beetled down over her slitted blue eyes. "It's been almost a week since Halloween. That's a lot of time to fill me in." She glanced at Rudy. "Oh, wait, I'm wrong. You've had your, um, *hands full* with other things, haven't you?"

I frowned. "Gwen, that's not fair. We had to do that."

"Had to what? *Fuck* him? Right there in the office?!"

"Actually, yeah."

"Wanna tell me why?"

I swallowed. "No."

Were those the beginning of tears in her eyes? Gwen *never* cried. "You're right. None of this is fair. It's not fair that you're going through this. It's not fair that I'm taking care of this shop all by myself. It's not fair that before them—" She pointed at Rudy. "—you could tell me anything. And now..."

I leaned on the counter, trying to sound reasonable. "Gwen, I'm not telling you because it could be dangerous."

She rounded on me. Those were tears in her eyes. Tears to go with the rage that she barely kept banked. "Obviously. If you've *killed* someone!"

I flinched. Rudy's hand rubbed my lower back.

"Gwen, a lot has happened—"

"Yeah. I get that." She took a deep breath. "You know what? Fuck it. Let's figure out a way that you can take care of the bills and stuff remotely so you don't have to come into the shop anymore."

"What?"

"Yeah. You obviously shouldn't be here. Whatever's going on, it's not likely to stop soon, right?"

I shook my head, blinking back more tears burning in my eyes.

Gwen swiped at her own eyes but kept her tone brisk. "I'm going to call and place an ad in the morning for some part-time help. You okay with that?"

I nodded miserably.

"Fine."

"Gwen…"

"Not now, Meg. You don't have the time and I don't have the patience." She trembled. "But we do need to talk. Eventually. If nothing else, to figure out what to do with the shop."

"Yeah. I know."

Chapter Six

The drive home was quiet and uneventful. Rudy took the wheel. I wasn't up for it. I leaned against the passenger door the whole way, staring morosely out the window at the passing traffic. He held my hand most of the time.

Home. Where was that, exactly? My sense of home had become distorted in the past week. Until recently, it was a nice little blue house where I lived alone with a bunch of trees. But I hadn't seen that place in a week now. Home had almost instantly become wherever two certain shifters were. Was that a good thing? I still barely knew them. But now it looked like the reason that I'd initially drawn them to me wasn't gone after all, so I couldn't even figure out *if* I wanted them around, because I really *had* to have them around.

We arrived at the house to find Michael's shiny black Jaguar out front. I followed Rudy despondently to the front door.

Michael opened it before we got to it and grabbed us both in a hug. He said nothing, just held on, and we echoed the sentiment. At least, I did. The feel of my big, strong cat together with the feel of my big, strong wolf made me feel much better, if not good. Tears sprang to my eyes and I ruthlessly tried to stop the flow.

He released us finally and led me to the couch. I sat and Michael knelt before me, smoothing my hair from my face. He used his thumb to wipe away a few tears that had escaped. "You okay?"

"No."

He pressed his lips to my temple. "Hungry?"

I sighed. "Yes."

"That I can fix," Rudy declared. He stepped back and rounded the counter that separated the kitchen from the main room. I watched as he opened the refrigerator to peer inside.

Michael continued to watch me. He'd changed out of his work clothes into worn jeans. Nothing else. His hair was down, lightly brushing those broad, muscular shoulders. I reached out to touch it, twining black silk around my fingers. He moved up onto the couch beside me, all feline grace despite his bulk, and twisted to face me. He took my hand and drew it into his lap. "Tell me what happened."

I did. As much as I knew. I told him about Chloe, who she was, what Roland knew and remembered about her. I told him what Chloe had said as well as what I'd drawn from Roland's memories confirming her words. He had, indeed, bequeathed everything he owned to his coven. It was a legal contract for both mundanes as well as the

Witches' Council. The legal papers didn't call the women a coven—it wouldn't do for a successful businessman to be seen calling himself a witch—but rather individual inheritors. It was the second piece of the legal papers, those only meant for the Witches' Council or enforcers, that made the belongings the joint ownership of the coven.

Even though he was busy cooking, I spoke loud enough so Rudy heard, not sure how much he'd caught when it had occurred.

I left out the part about Gwen, not ready to think about that.

When I was talked out, Michael smoothed a hand over my shoulder. Strong fingers landed at the nape of my neck and started to gently massage. "I don't feel the power surge. Are you okay now? The memories?"

"Yeah. I was doing fine. Just…" I shrugged, biting my lip to try and stave off yet more tears.

Without another word, he drew me into his arms and into a kiss. It was a beautiful thing. All soft lips and sympathy. I clung to him and let him guide me, but neither of us was in any kind of hurry.

"Should I put dinner on hold?"

We parted gently at the sound of Rudy's voice. Michael looked at me, reaching up to brush bangs from my face. "No. Let's eat. We need to decide what to do."

So we discussed it over a simple meal of pork chops and cheesy potatoes. We weighed the merits of not going, but that seemed a bad idea. True, they could go to Shannon at any time, but they seemed less likely to go if I at least played their game. Rudy brought up the idea of going to Shannon ourselves, but I nixed that idea. If we gave Shannon any fodder against me, she'd use it. They even mentioned skipping town. That one threw me for a loop, that Michael and Rudy casually talked about leaving the house they'd just purchased. But that part didn't seem to bother either of them, and I eventually attributed it to the fact that since they'd just moved there, they didn't have any deep attachment.

In the end, we kept coming back to the same conclusion. To really figure out and deal with what was happening, we had to go to Roland's house and see for ourselves.

We finished dinner, and I helped Rudy clean up while Michael disappeared into his office. Rudy and I didn't talk much, but it wasn't one of those uncomfortable silences. It was more like we were both talked out and just enjoyed a few moments of quiet.

I must have been nodding off, though, because as I was finishing, Rudy quite firmly took the dishtowel from my hand, set it on the counter, then steered me out of the kitchen toward the hall.

"Where are we going?" I asked over a yawn.

"To bed."

I blinked. We were going to Roland's house tomorrow. Which meant that Michael probably thought it would be best to "strengthen our bond." Translation: sex. I almost groaned at the thought.

Rudy propelled me toward the bathroom, then left, presumably to finish up in the kitchen. I went about my nightly ritual. When I emerged into the bedroom, neither of my lovers was there. I yawned hard enough to hear my jaw crack. I shuffled across the hall briefly to fetch a blanket, then returned to the master bedroom and curled up underneath it. My thought was to get some shut-eye before either of the shifters arrived.

I woke, groggy, in a swelter of heat. I tried to turn, only to find myself tangled in a blanket and trapped between two heavy bodies.

A pair of hands helped me to remove the blanket, then urged me to lie back down against the warm, bare back that was there.

I twisted my neck and blinked, trying to focus bleary eyes on Michael. "Don't we need to have sex?"

"No. You need sleep."

"But…"

"Sleep."

I sighed and turned back to cuddle against Rudy's back, in no shape to argue.

Chapter Seven

"What can you tell us about these women?"

I sat in the passenger seat of Michael's car while Michael drove. Rudy was stretched across the backseat. I stared straight ahead and put my hand on Michael's knee. If I was going to delve into memories, I had to touch one of them. I heard Rudy shift, then felt his hands reach up to rest on my shoulders. The fingers of one hand started to gently massage my nape.

I sifted through Roland's memories, trying not to delve too deeply. "Aggie's the one to look out for. She'll be the ballsy Nordic blonde who acts like she owns the place. As far as she's concerned, she was Roland's right hand. She wasn't, but he let her believe it. She's a lawyer, but she's not his main lawyer. That'd be Thomas Blackwell. Aggie's the only one who knew she was a witch before Roland found her, but she only got her gifts from her father's side, so they're kind of weak.

"Chloe's the one who came to the shop yesterday. I doubt seriously we need to worry about her. I'm guessing she's the one who came because she's the weakest.

"Deidre's the homebody. Quiet, mousey little woman with long brown hair. Great cook and very into food. Not at all interested in magic and pretty much keeps to herself as much as she can. She and Chloe are good friends." I grimaced. "She also had an affair going with Brent."

"Brent?" Rudy asked, a growl lacing his words. "Roland's leashed wolf?"

"Yeah." I looked at Michael's profile. "What happened to him?"

He shrugged. "He and Rudy fought on Halloween."

Rudy propped his chin on the back of my seat, draping one arm over the opposite side and over my shoulder and front. "I hurt him, but when the circle dropped, my first priority was getting to you. I don't know what happened to him."

I reached up to caress his jaw in brief thanks.

I sighed. "Hannah is Aggie's buddy and an incredibly prissy little bitch. Not very bright, though. She and Aggie run the house, but they don't *do* anything, really. Then there's Melissa. She's not as quiet and shy as Chloe or Deidre, but she's not as bad as Aggie or Hannah. She spends most of her time in the gardens. She's an herbalist and has been getting more into it since Roland introduced her to witchcraft."

"So Aggie and Hannah are likely the ones to watch."

I nodded. "From what I know. The others would happily back out if they could. Of course, getting a part of Roland's estate might change their minds some. But none of them are strong enough or mean-spirited enough to cause harm."

Michael took in all of this information without comment.

I stared at his profile for a few moments. "So, what do we do?"

He didn't even turn. "Why are you asking me?"

I frowned. "You're usually the one with the plan."

"I wouldn't want to presume to tell you what to do."

I closed my eyes and ground my teeth for a brief moment. "Michael, please."

He said nothing for a moment, then sighed. "We need to stick together. It's important that we don't get split up."

Rudy asked for me. "Why?"

"Who knows what being in that house will do to Roland's memories? Meg, it would be a good idea if you try and touch at least one of us at all times."

I shivered. Not that touching them was such a hardship. Just the fact that I *needed* to do so. Like he said, who knew what being in a place where many of the recent events in Roland's life had occurred would do to me?

"Other than that, I'm not certain there's anything we can plan. We don't know if there's a hidden agenda behind their wanting you to come to the house. My guess is, there is. Otherwise, they would be amenable to meeting you somewhere else. But you say she was adamant about you coming to the house?"

I nodded.

"She seemed pretty set on it, yeah," Rudy confirmed.

"She really wanted me to come last night."

Michael nodded. "It's probably a good thing that you didn't. But that also means that they had last night and this morning to prepare further."

"Should we not have called to let them know we were coming?" I asked.

Michael shrugged. "I don't know that it would make a difference. Whatever they've got planned, it's ready."

"So we're walking into an ambush?'

"Most likely. But then, they don't know what we know."

"What do we know?"

"That you've got Roland's memory and power. That should work to our advantage, even if it's the one thing we want to hide." He paused, thinking. "Meg, you've said that Roland didn't share his magics. I'm assuming he has a storehouse of power in that house?"

"Not so much a storehouse, but he's got set magics. The standard stuff like shields, sealings, and warnings. Two permanent circles. But they were all tied to him and designed to diffuse without his personal influence, even if it was only occasionally." I dropped my head forward, rubbing my forehead. "It really scares me that I know all this. Some of the memories are starting to feel like they're mine."

Rudy squeezed my shoulder. Michael reached for my free hand and held it on his thigh.

We arrived at the pretentious entrance to Roland's estate. The opening in the brick wall was normally barred by the huge wrought-iron double gates, but the gates stood open. The smooth driveway extended up a moderately steep incline to curve in front of the house and back in on itself. Two massive trees flanked the house, shadowing the bushes and fences that hid the side and back yards from view. The brick walls that surrounded the property edged the sizeable front yard, tall enough to obscure any view of the neighbors. The house itself had twelve bedrooms, each with an adjoining bathroom, as well as a living room, a game room, a formal dining room, and a sitting room. There was a pool out back and a huge manicured garden around one side and back. A densely wooded area extended down a hill behind the property.

Michael pulled into the driveway and went all around the circle, past the carport full of cars, to position the Jag facing out. Ready for a quick getaway.

My stomach turned. I sank into the seat. "Do we really have to do this?"

Michael just got out of the car.

I grimaced at his back and got out.

Rudy caught me before we went anywhere and briefly hugged me. He slid his hand down to twine his fingers with mine and led me to the back of the car to stand beside Michael, looking up at the house.

"Do you sense anything unusual?" Michael asked.

I took quick stock of our surroundings, not sure what I was looking for. I risked a brief allowance of Roland's memories, figuring they'd crop up if anything was amiss. I shrugged. "Not anything obvious."

Michael nodded. "Let's go. Stay close. Stay calm." Without looking back at us, Michael led the way up a short, paved walkway to the house. When we weren't close enough behind him, he shot us a glance over his shoulder and slowed his steps. I followed him up the two porch steps, keeping a death grip on Rudy's hand. I felt the niggling of the memories and flits of scenes from the past skittering through my mind, but nothing too overpowering yet.

Yet.

Michael stopped just before the door and turned, his mouth open to say something. What, I don't know because the door opened and he snapped back around, placing himself between me and the person at the door.

I peeked over his shoulder. It was Aggie Nilsen. She stood tall, slim, and immaculately perfect in her fitted blue dress and high-heeled shoes. Her platinum blonde hair was swept back into a chignon, and I wouldn't be surprised if the sapphires dangling from her ears were real. She made me feel scruffy.

She looked over Michael, noting him as one might note an underling, then focused on me. "Ms. Grey. How nice of you to join us." She stepped aside and swept her arm. "Please come in."

Michael passed by her first, and the mere fact that she didn't take the opportunity to ogle him convinced me that I didn't like her. As if I didn't know it already. But no sane woman could have that man that close to her and not at least look. Not unless she wasn't into guys, but I happened to recall that Aggie and Roland…

Avoiding that thought, I followed Michael, still clutching Rudy's hand. Trying to banish memories of Aggie having sex with Roland from my mind, I was halfway across the marble entry hall before I felt the clap of a spell closing behind me.

Gasping, I whirled, looking at the door. Aggie stood there, having just closed it. I met her cold, blue-eyed stare. "What's with the spell?"

She blinked. "I beg your pardon?"

I frowned. "Yeah. You should. What's with the confinement spell?"

Rudy growled, squeezing my hand, and Michael closed in on my other side, slightly behind me. I was aware of both of them casting their gazes around the stark, cold room, but I kept mine trained on Aggie.

She raised her arm and extended it toward the arched entry to the black and chrome living room. "If you'd care to join us, we can explain everything."

I sneered at her as she proceeded to walk through the entryway herself. "What's with the spell?"

I needn't have asked. We followed her and I stopped short underneath the arch, just at the edge of two curved steps that led down to the room's plush white carpeting.

Across the room, right in front of the beveled French doors that led to the patio, in a large, uncomfortable-looking chair, sat Shannon Cavanagh, the grand dame of the Southwest United States.

I did mention that she and I were teenage rivals and that she's never forgiven me for being stronger than her? Yeah, I think I did.

"Shannon." I said it as a statement of fact, trying to make myself believe what I was seeing. Because I didn't *want* to believe what I was seeing.

She smiled that false smile that never, ever made it to her blue eyes. "Meg."

"Fancy meeting you here."

What the hell was going on? Shannon sat in one of the half-dozen black leather and chrome chairs, looking prim and proper in her cream slacks and navy blouse. Pearls ringed her neck and wrists, and single drops dangled from her ears. Two guys who I could only think of as goons stood behind her, each looking the stereotypical muscular bodyguard. I could tell they were shifters, but not what kind. Another man in a sharp silver-gray suit stood to the side, fingers resting on a briefcase that sat on the shiny metallic table beside him. A cursory look told me that he was human and had some gifts but might not be a full-fledged witch. He looked familiar, but I couldn't immediately place him. Hannah and Melissa were seated on the couch near the fireplace, each looking as though they'd been told to stay put. Deidre sat in a chair across the room, her eyes averted. Chloe sat in a chair beside her and met my gaze with big, soulful brown eyes and a painfully apologetic look on her doll face. Aggie had taken up stance beside the fireplace, as near as she could get to Shannon without looking like she was toadying.

Michael growled and Rudy spun. I cast a glance over my shoulder toward the dining area to see no less than five more goons—all shifters—emerging to fill the hallway behind us. Beyond the glass of the French doors, three more were visible.

One good thing about this. Not one of Roland's memories threatened to overwhelm me. Oh, they were there, but my own roiling emotions took precedence. Potent things, fear and anger. My childhood and teenage nemesis sat before me, and I had a whopper of a secret to hide.

I turned back to Shannon and fought to keep my cool. "Is all this necessary?"

"You'll have to tell me if it is, Meg."

"I came at the request of the ladies here."

She smoothed a hand over the knee she had crossed over her other leg. "Mmm, yes. Your coven."

"They're not my coven."

"But they're linked to you."

Think fast, Meg. "That was Roland's doing. You've heard of Roland, haven't you? The one who took over these women and used their magic? The one who was trying to bully me and take me over?"

"Yes. I've heard of Roland Parks. I'm rather upset this wasn't reported to me before his death." She narrowed her gaze at me. "Why didn't you call me, Meg? It seems you'd known him for months."

"How was I to know you didn't know about him?"

"Why didn't you report that he threatened you?"

"I didn't think you'd help."

"Despite our past, it is my duty as grand dame to investigate these matters and see that they don't happen."

I nodded nicely. "I'm sorry, then. I took our personal history to heart." She was lying out her ass. She would've done anything to avoid getting me out of trouble, but she could say whatever she wanted now without reprisals.

"Mmm. And now we have a situation. The witch is dead and it looks as if you killed him. With magic." She speared me with her gaze. "Did you?"

I hoped like hell that I looked as calm as I wasn't. "It was self-defense. He had me in a circle."

"Self-defense. Really?"

"You don't believe me?"

"The evidence *is* rather stacked against you."

I shrugged, kind of surprised that I still had a death grip on Rudy's hand. *Stay calm*, Michael had said. I was doing my best. "Then it doesn't matter what I say."

"I'd like to hear your side of the story."

Finally Michael spoke up, his deep voice a pleasant interruption. "Shouldn't a formal interrogation take place before a tribunal?"

Shocked, I looked up at him. What the hell was he doing?

Her cool gaze switched to him, annoyance clear in her lowered brows. "*Senhor* Sandoval. I'm surprised to see you here."

I glanced at Shannon. They'd met?

He nodded at her. "Grand Dame."

"How quickly situations change."

"Indeed."

I glanced from one to the other. Something was going on here that I didn't know about. What was with the "*senhor*" stuff?

"I had hoped that you would consider my generous offer."

"I did, Grand Dame. But a shifter can hardly deny a guardian spell when it calls to him."

What offer?! I so wanted to ask, but I didn't dare.

Shannon turned a cold frown to me. "Meg, I congratulate you on leashing one of Alessandro D'Cruz's shifter's."

I tried to hide my frown. Alessandro D'Cruz. I knew that name. Why? My own memories weren't forthcoming with details and I was afraid to delve too deeply into Roland's.

Shannon uncrossed her legs and sat back in her chair. Her hands looked casual as they perched on the arms of the chair, until her fingers wrapped around the chrome. I don't think she was aware of it. Something had happened. Shannon's normally cool exterior had been cracked by Michael's presence. That she hadn't expected him was obvious, but who *was* he that my leashing him made her mad?

She eyed Rudy, her vision slightly off, which told me she was looking magically instead of purely visually. "And you must be *Senhor* Sandoval's wolf companion. Meg, you've leashed them *both?*"

Obviously. "Yes. It was rather sudden." I almost laughed, wondering why I said that. Okay, I was on the edge of hysteria. Hysteria was bad. Must return to the calm. I took a deep breath.

Her glance at Aggie was brief, but it was enough to tell me that she was pissed at the other woman. Hadn't Aggie mentioned who my shifters were? Come to think of it, could Aggie have known? Not likely. Roland hadn't known. But I didn't think Shannon was going to be very forgiving of her ignorance.

"Indeed." She squeezed the arms of the chair again, then visibly—to me, at least—gathered her composure. "Well..." She waved an arm toward the couch that remained vacant. "...please sit and tell me the story of what happened here on Samhain."

Michael grabbed my arm, keeping me from stepping further into the room.

It gained him Shannon's instant attention. "Is there a problem, *Senhor* Sandoval?"

Michael kept his hold on my arm. "I believe I must insist that any further questioning be conducted before a tribunal."

"*You* must insist?" Shannon glanced coolly at me.

I shrugged. "Works for me."

Her left brow lifted as she returned her attention to Michael. "This is not a formal interrogation, *Senhor* Sandoval."

"It very likely should be."

"And why is that?" Shannon asked. "Is your witch guilty?"

Yes, I caught the reference to me as "his witch," but I let it go. One, I didn't especially mind, and two, I knew Michael was much better at this sort of thing than I was. I'd leave the talking to him.

He inclined his head in seeming deference. "Forgive me, Grand Dame, but Meg has made me aware of the personal history between the two of you. Given that, would it not look better for all concerned if other, disinterested parties were present?"

The man in the silver suit's interest perked up. He took a step forward, his cool, black gaze darting from Michael to Shannon. Finally a shadow of one of Roland's memories identified him for me: Thomas Blackwell, Roland's lawyer.

Shannon narrowed her eyes at Michael. "Are you implying that I wouldn't be impartial?"

"I don't know you personally, Grand Dame, but from what I've heard of your history, I would say that it would be difficult for you to be impartial."

"How dare you!"

"He's right, Shannon," I piped in, finally seeing where he was going. Goddess, he was smart! And how did he know witches' laws so well? "Everyone knows you hate me. You'll be looking for a way to get me."

She pounded a fist on the arm of her chair, echoes of the foot she'd always stomped when we were kids. "I'm grand dame of the Southwest United States. It's my duty to investigate these matters and protect the magically gifted."

"Indeed, Grand Dame—" How did Michael keep his voice just slightly deferential without giving in? "— and in matters of accusations of murder, it is often in the best interest of all parties concerned if the entire story waits for a tribunal."

He was, of course, exactly right. Many grand dames and wizards wouldn't bother with a tribunal and didn't need to. If they didn't know the parties concerned and didn't have a personal interest, the grand leaders served perfectly well as judge and jury. But in instances where they *were* personally involved or had any piece of a personal stake, a tribunal of three grand leaders or respected representatives was called for. She could deny we made the request, and she could maybe even sway the witnesses present, but that had its own problems. The people she'd quieted would all know and thus have a hold on her. Plus, it'd look bad if she killed me, given our history, even if she had cause.

Shannon sucked a slow breath in through her nostrils. "Very well, *Senhor* Sandoval. You have made your point. I shall call a tribunal." She stood and turned to me. She just managed not to smirk. "You do realize that this means I'll need to confine you."

Shit. I looked at the ceiling and glanced over my shoulder toward the front door. "Looks like you've already done that." I turned back to her, matching her not-quite-glare. "The spell is your work, I take it?"

She didn't bother to answer. Everyone knew it was. The coven wasn't nearly strong enough or organized enough to keep me confined. Plus, if they really were linked to me, I'd have felt it. No, Shannon was the only one around with enough juice to first hide the spell from me, then trigger it and even hope to hold me.

The goons came from behind her chair to take their places at her back as she stepped closer to the three of us. She gave Michael a searching gaze before resting her attention on me again. "Margaret Grey, you are to stay in this house until further notice. Any attempt on your part to break the confinement spell or to leave the premises will be seen as the act of a guilty party."

I nodded. Standard fare. I'd seen and heard my mother do this a number of times. I didn't like it, but at least I was alive, with the chance to face a tribunal. That was, at least, a chance.

"Your shifters may leave the premises, but only in the presence of one of my people or an enforcer. I will leave a number stationed here and send for a few more. It shouldn't take more than a week to gather the tribunal."

"A week?"

We all turned to look at Aggie. I was actually kind of shocked that she'd stayed silent this long. We were, after all, talking about what she considered to be *her* property.

Shannon arched a brow at her. "Ms. Nilsen?"

Aggie bowed her head briefly. "Forgive me, Grand Dame, but are you saying that this woman and her companions will be staying here for up to a week?"

"Yes. And why shouldn't they? Hasn't Mr. Blackwell stated that the house belongs to the coven?" Shannon tilted her head slightly to the side. "By rights, the house belongs more to her, as the strongest and most skilled, than to you, does it not?"

I blinked, not sure what Shannon was doing. Was she miffed at Aggie and so felt the need to tweak her? Or was she setting me up as the bad guy in Aggie's eyes? Neither was necessary. She was just stirring the pot.

Aggie tried really hard not to scowl, but didn't succeed. "The house belongs to *all* of us."

Shannon nodded. "Indeed. So you won't mind if she stays here while we await the tribunal."

Hannah shot to her feet, pointing at me. "But she killed him!"

Aha! Now I knew where the accusation had come from. Bitch.

Shannon narrowed her eyes at Hannah, who visibly blanched. "That has yet to be proven."

Oh! That must have hurt!

Aggie stepped forward, almost in front of Hannah, clearly trying to block her. "Grand Dame, with all due respect, this creates quite an uncomfortable situation."

"And yet everyone involved is an adult and can conduct themselves accordingly. It's quite a large house, Ms. Nilsen. I'm sure you can avoid one another. I assure you I shall assemble a tribunal as quickly as possible. I will make it known to the other grand leaders that an extended delay will cause you difficulty."

I almost laughed. It was so nice to see that bitchiness directed somewhere else other than at me. At a deserving target, no less.

Aggie's eyes went wide; then she bowed her head again. "Forgive me, Grand Dame. We will, of course, do as you say."

"Thank you." Shannon turned back to me. Again her gaze flicked to Michael. No doubt she was peeved that I had someone who thought fast on my side. "Meg, I'll need your cell number." She held out a hand to the side and one of the goons put a business card into it. She held it out to me. "This is a number where you can reach my assistant if you need to get in touch with me."

I nodded, then gave my cell number to one of the goons, who stored it directly in his phone.

Once that was done, Shannon turned to Roland's lawyer. "Mr. Blackwell, you're free to stay and discuss matters with this coven as you like. I wouldn't imagine any dealings can be finalized until after the tribunal has met and decided."

He stepped forward, bobbing his head with a grin. His black hair was slicked with either goop or hairspray, because it didn't budge. "That will be fine, Grand Dame. If Ms. Grey doesn't mind, I'd like to talk with her briefly to fill her in on the details of Mr. Parks's will."

I nearly groaned, but managed to stifle it. I hated legal stuff.

Shannon looked at me again. "It's quite an inheritance, Meg. I hope you're innocent and free to enjoy it."

I grimaced. "I don't want it."

Yet again, Shannon's gaze flicked to Michael. "I will never understand you."

With that, she left.

Chapter Eight

I envied Rudy. He got to leave Roland's estate to go back to the house and pick up clothes and stuff for us. True, he had one of Shannon's shifters with him, but he had to be having a better time than me.

As lawyers went, Thomas Blackwell was passable. He was a personable man with a ready smile, even if you could tell—ok, *I* could tell—that he couldn't be trusted. From both flashes of Roland's memories as well as my own assessment, I knew that the more money Thomas Blackwell's client had, the better he served them. Roland had been one of his best clients. For at least an hour, he talked me through stacks of paperwork and legalese. Michael sat with us and actually did most of the talking and asking of questions. He seemed to understand most of it. After the first half-hour, the men pretty much ignored my presence altogether. Which was just as well. I couldn't keep track of what they were saying.

Aggie and Hannah hovered in the dusky shadows of the next room but didn't join us in the dining room. At one point, I heard them in a hissing argument. Deidre appeared twice briefly, first to offer to make us sandwiches, then to deliver them. I hadn't a clue where Melissa and Chloe disappeared to.

Surprisingly, Roland's memories left me pretty much alone. It might have been my own stress level. Or the fact that there were just too many memories. I hated to think that the reason might be that I was getting used to them.

At long last, Thomas—as he insisted we call him—let us go. As we were standing up from the table, Chloe appeared in the doorway, her hands clutched before her.

"A-are you finished?"

"Yes, we are, Chloe," Thomas said, smiling at her.

She didn't see it, her face tilted down. Fine blonde bangs obscured her face. "I-I'm to see Meg and her...um—" She stopped, glancing up at Michael.

He didn't growl, but it was a close thing. "My name is Michael. Use it."

She shivered. "I'm to see Meg and Michael to their rooms."

So why was she nervous? I found out when she led us upstairs.

I stood just inside the doorway, scowling. "Chloe, whose rooms are these?" I knew, but I couldn't very well tell her.

"Y-yours."

"Whose were they *before?*"

She edged another step away from me. "Roland's."

"Oh, *hell* no! Whose twisted idea was that?"

"I'm sorry!" She backed up against a wall, right beside an open doorway that led to an adjacent bedroom. "I-it's the only set of rooms that can accommodate all three of you. We assumed you'd want to be together."

You'd think I was the shifter by the way I growled. "There's got to be a better option."

"Meg." This from Michael, who had walked the perimeter of the rooms and peered through all four doors to see what lay beyond. He looked at me. "Beyond the rooms having been Roland's, is there a problem with staying here?"

I gaped at him. *Other than Roland's memories?!* But I couldn't say that. "Other than it's fucking creepy?"

He watched me steadily. "But they're very likely the best rooms in the house." He turned to Chloe. "With the biggest bed?"

She blinked and nodded.

He turned back to me and shrugged. "The three of us aren't going to be comfortable sleeping anywhere else."

And, with that, he'd just confirmed I was sleeping with both of them. Yay. Now they knew I was a slut. I crossed my arms under my breasts and glared at him, unable to come up with a retort fast enough.

He put his hand on Chloe's shoulder, making her jump a mile at the contact. "We'll stay. Would you mind leaving us alone now?"

"Michael!"

He ignored me, busy smiling at Chloe as he urged her toward the open door just behind me. She fell for the charm, some of her fear easing away. "O-of course."

"And you'll let Rudy know where we are when he returns?"

"Y-yes."

He grinned and she melted. Not that she had a chance. I had yet to keep my skin from tingling when he smiled at me like that.

I stepped aside as he ushered Chloe to the door.

She stopped just as they came up beside me. "I'm so sorry," she said. She reached out to touch my arm, but pulled it back when I flinched away. "For everything." She left.

Michael shut the door.

I punched his arm after he closed the door on her. "What the hell...?"

He grabbed me, slapping a hand over my mouth. I was manhandled into the middle of the room, one brawny arm pinning me to his massive chest. I screamed, making sure he knew I was pissed.

Judging by the look in his eyes, he knew and accepted that. "This is probably also the most secure room in the house," he murmured, lips hovering over the hand he still had over my mouth. Those green eyes bore into mine, melting a good chunk of my ire away. "Did Roland have a sealing spell on these rooms?"

I blinked at him, the rest of my anger draining away. The knowledge came readily, and I nodded.

"Good." He slid his hand from my mouth and loosely wrapped both arms around my waist, pulling me flush against that wonderfully hard body of his. "Can you activate it?"

I considered, then nodded.

He smiled. "Good." He brushed his lips against mine. "Do it."

I caught his bottom lip with my teeth, nipping lightly. The perverse part of me wanted to argue, but I got where he was going now. "I can't when you're distracting me."

He sighed. "Pity." He pulled back from me, and I watched as he started to make another, slower circuit of the room, opening all the drawers and looking behind everything. "The spell, Meg," he reminded without looking at me.

"Bastard," I muttered, then closed my eyes.

A sealing spell is just that. It's a kind of bubble that you can put around an area. There are different types. Shannon's containment spell was a form of one, designed to seal me within the house. The spell on Roland's rooms was actually simpler, focused purely on sound. Once active, anyone inside the room could hear normally both in and out of the spell, but no one outside the spell could hear anything that went on within it. Best part about it was that there weren't any incantations to learn. Well, there was to initially set the spell, but once it was set, it only took a thought from the spellcaster to activate it. The spell flared to life easily for me. I opened my eyes and saw the soft blue haze around the room through magical vision. The spell recognized me, little tendrils of it flaring brighter as I drifted toward one of the walls. Rather, it recognized the power I'd stolen from Roland. I wasn't too sure I was happy about that.

I skewed my vision back to normal and turned, then jumped to find Michael right at my side, almost touching my shoulder. When had he come up behind me? "It's done."

His eyes bored into mine. "What kind of seal is it?"

I frowned. "Just sound. What?"

"Nothing." He stepped back and the intensity of his gaze went down a few notches. He brushed his fingers over my shoulder. "How far does it extend?"

"The boundaries are the walls of this suite, including both bedrooms, the bathroom, and sitting room."

He nodded and turned, looking toward the open door to the other bedroom. "Is this for his mistress?"

I shook my head and went to the bay window. The sun had set and night was encroaching. Dusky lavender shadows crept across the side garden. "Kind of. Those were supposed to be my rooms."

"Ah." I heard the door shut. Only the leash let me know that he approached me, because he sure as heck didn't make any noise. He slid his arms around me from behind. "He's dead, Meg."

"Is he? All of his memories are sitting in my head. This house *knows* me. His coven is mine." I clutched at the strong arms banded beneath my breasts. "Goddess, Michael, I'm starting to not be able to tell the difference between his memories and mine."

A warm nose nudged aside the hair covering my ear, baring my neck to the soft lips that caressed it. "But you're not him. You're just adjusting to your newfound power."

"It's not mine."

"It is now."

Tears burned in my eyes. "I don't want it. I don't want any of this."

He nipped my earlobe. "*Any* of it?"

I closed my eyes, sinking back into him. It was impossible not to enjoy his touch. "*Most* of it."

"Mmmm." He turned me around, tilting my head up so that I could see those gorgeous eyes. "Let me see if I can help distract you from the rest."

I went willingly into his kiss, all for letting him take my cares away.

He walked backwards to the bed, kissing me all the way. He fell back on the plush gold and brown patterned duvet, taking me with him.

I draped myself over him, determined to ignore that this was Roland's bed and determined to beat down his disgusting memories of what had occurred there. I framed Michael's face with my hands, eating at his mouth. He took it all, responding but not taking the initiative. Letting me drive. Soon I was itching to have more. I pushed up just enough to slide my hands down his torso until I could grab the hem of his pullover and yank it up. Warm, beautiful skin under my hands. I shoved the pullover higher until I could get my mouth on his chest, nipping at the sparse mat of hair, lapping at the chiseled edge of muscles, then finally biting down on his nipple.

He moaned, struggling beneath me to remove his shirt. His legs moved, and I could only hope he was toeing off his shoes.

I spanned my hands over the firm muscles that covered his ribs and simply marveled at the satin strength of him. All of our arguments and troubles from the past few days flew from my mind. Everything went away except for this burning need to have this man.

I sat on his thighs so I could work on his pants. He helped me, then obligingly lifted his hips so I could take pants and underwear with me as I backed off the bed.

He lay propped on his elbows, watching me while I tossed aside his clothes, then scrambled at mine. That marvelous, huge cock of his lay at half-mast against his belly.

Well, that kind of pissed me off. Here I was all wet and gushy, and he was half hard? That would never do. I got my pants, shoes, and panties off, but couldn't be bothered to take the time to remove my top and bra. I pounced back on the bed, landing between his thighs.

"Eager, are we?" he teased, a small grin tilting the corners of his mouth.

I glared up at him, then lowered my head to lap at the heavy sacs that hung below his cock. "You should be nice to the woman with her teeth near your dick."

He chuckled. "Yes, ma'am."

I nodded. "That's more like it."

And with that, I commenced to feasting. There was a lot of flesh, after all. His balls were warm and furry, soft and firm at the same time. And his cock...I couldn't hope to get my entire mouth around that monster, so I had to spend time licking and lapping at it, determined not to miss tasting any of it. By the time I started seriously sucking on the tip of him, he was no longer at half-mast. I wrapped both hands around him and sucked for all I was worth, determined to blow his mind.

"Meg!" His fingers tangled in my hair. His hips twitched.

Oh, yeah! I stopped.

He groaned, almost growled.

"Hold on, big guy," I grumbled, climbing up on top of him. "I'm not done with you yet."

He sneered, grabbing my hips.

I giggled, taking hold of that cock, positioning it, then letting gravity do its thing.

Well, until Michael decided that gravity was too slow and yanked down on my hips.

I hissed. Even wet as I was, he was too damn big for me to get seated in one shove. It took three. I froze, hovering over him, just enjoying the feeling of it. The only time this was better was when Rudy was with us.

Fingers digging into my waist forced me to lift. The hips that shoved at me as I fell back pushed a moan out of me. That did it. I couldn't stay still any longer. I leaned back, bracing my hands on Michael's powerful thighs, and rode him for all I was worth.

I came first, shuddering and gasping as my body clutched his.

He waited until it had passed over me before rolling us over. I landed like a rag doll beneath him, and he didn't mind one bit. He situated himself, then pounded another orgasm out of me before he let himself go.

Fabulous sex and the disturbing events of the day wore me out. It's the only reason I can fathom for the fact that I fell promptly to sleep.

Chapter Nine

Rudy was back. Even before I opened my eyes, I knew he was nearby. Michael was also nearby, but not in the same room.

I rolled over and peered over a mound of pillows sheathed in lemon silk to see Rudy sitting at the writing desk, eyes glued to the laptop before him.

He glanced up, grinning. "You finally awake?"

I yawned and sat up, letting the light blanket that covered me drop to my waist. I was completely naked now. Either Michael or Rudy must have stripped off my shirt and bra before he tucked me in. "What time is it?"

"Nine."

"Wow, I slept that long?" I think it had been around five by the time Michael finished with me.

"Yep. You hungry?"

"A little."

He stood, stretching. His long, lean body wore only jeans and his unlaced Converse shoes, exposing his shapely torso and arms to my appreciative gaze. "I'll go get you something to eat."

"You don't have to."

He grinned, kneeling on the bed beside me. "No worries. Michael and I already ate. They've got some keeping warm for you downstairs." He dropped a kiss on my lips. "Won't take a minute."

"Where's Michael?" I asked as he sauntered to the door.

He pointed. "He found a hidden room."

I turned as he exited. Just as I saw the bookcase ajar, Roland's memories told me of the existence of the hidden room. I also knew what it housed and realized why it fascinated Michael.

I padded over to the bookcase and stood in the opening. Michael sat before a bank of security monitors. Depending on how you set them, the little black and white screens showed what was happening in every room of the house, the pool house, the gardening shed, and the four corners of the outside walls.

"I'm impressed," Michael mused, knowing I was there. "He's got quite a setup here."

I hugged myself. Roland had loved this place. No one else knew about it. "Yeah. How'd you find it?"

"Detective work."

"Ah."

He glanced over his shoulder. "You okay?"

I nodded, but didn't bother to turn up the glum twist of my lips. "I'm gonna take a shower."

He nodded and turned back to the monitors.

I wandered into the big bathroom and made use of the utilitarian shower. It was clean and on the large side, but it didn't have any character. Kind of like the bed in the other room. With the exception of the plush mattress and silk sheets, Roland hadn't furnished his home for comfort. In that, it wasn't so much a "home" as a place where he'd lived and showed off.

Thankfully, his memories continued to simmer just beyond my conscious thoughts, just like my own memories. Gah! Perish the thought.

Showered, I emerged from the bathroom dressed only in a big yellow towel. Rudy was back and had set a full plate of salmon, potatoes, and green beans on the desk beside him.

"Gwen called," he told me as I sat. He pushed my cell phone toward me. "I answered it. I saw that it was the shop and thought she might feel better to hear that you were okay."

I smiled grimly. "Thanks." I left the cell phone where it was and dug into my dinner.

Such a mess. Ever since Roland set his sights on me, my life hadn't been the same. Until him, I'd been very happy with the delusion that I could forget I was a powerful witch. But it wasn't meant to be. As the sixth daughter of the grand dame of the Northeast, I wasn't destined for a quiet life.

Michael emerged from the security cubby. Relaxed jeans hugged his waist and legs, and a red shirt hung unbuttoned across his chest and shoulders, the arms rolled up over his elbows. He padded barefooted across the room to a closed chest that had a big gym bag on top of it. He lifted it to look underneath. "Rudy, did you bring my laptop?"

Without taking his eyes from his computer screen, Rudy reached down near his legs and hefted a laptop case. "You mean this?"

"Ah!" Michael came to retrieve it, dropping a quick kiss on Rudy's cheek as he did. "You do take good care of me."

Rudy hummed happily without taking his eyes off his typing.

I chewed slowly as I watched Michael cross the room to drop down on the bed. He didn't bother to turn on the lamp, so he sat in what kind of looked like a dark cave created by the shadows of the heavy posts that stood at the four corners of the bed. He got his computer out and fired it up. I glanced at Rudy's screen to see some sort of internet forum that he seemed intent on following. They must have hooked into Roland's wireless. Roland had had both a wireless and a more secured network for some of his shadier work.

"Who are you guys?"

They both froze, then looked at me.

Okay, it was a strange question to ask of the two men you'd had sex with repeatedly for the past week, but seriously. I glanced from one to the other, gradually frowning. "I mean it. Who are you?" I pointed my fork at Michael. "And why did she call you '*senhor*'? And who's

Alessandro D'Cruz? And why is Shannon all hot for you? And when the *hell* did you and Shannon meet?"

He raised a brow. "Which question do you want answered?"

"All of them." I considered. "When did you meet Shannon?"

"It's customary for shifters to let the local authorities know they're moving to town."

"They don't normally meet the grand dame herself."

He shrugged. "She requested to meet me."

"I knew you were some sort of witch tracker and a private detective, but she acted like you were a lot more than that."

"I am." Why did I get the feeling there was more meaning to those two simple words than an answer to my question?

"Why didn't you tell me you knew her?"

"I don't know her. I've met her. And it didn't occur to me that you wouldn't realize we'd met." His voice was calm as a cat lying in the sun.

I grimaced. He was going to make me work for this. He'd probably distracted me earlier on purpose, hoping not to have this conversation. He'd been avoiding telling me about his past since we met. "Fine. My bad, then. Is Alessandro D'Cruz the witch that leashed you before?"

"Yes."

"Who was he?"

"You don't know?" He was really surprised, not just being sarcastic.

"Should I?"

"Yes. You should." He all but rolled his eyes as he typed something on his keyboard. "He was the grand wizard of Southern Brazil."

I blinked. Memories—mine and Roland's—surfaced to verify this. "He was supposed to be some kind of scientist or something. He died in one of his laboratories. An explosion or something."

"Is that your memory?"

"Not entirely."

He glanced up only briefly from the laptop. "Well, it's accurate. Alessandro was obsessed with biology and genealogy, but only as they pertained to shifters. He had a whole team of lab workers in his facilities; all of the workers were witches with degrees in science. He ensured their loyalty by fully supporting their community. Many of his researchers had been put through college by him."

"Impressive." Depending on personal philosophies, witches were either for or against science in general. Diehard old-schoolers saw science as a "new study" that got in the way of magic. More modern thinkers saw science as another form of magic. A dangerous one, because it could be learned by anyone, not just those born with magical gifts. It was quite odd for any witch—especially a grand wizard—to devote time and money to such a thing. "He was studying shifters? Scientifically?"

"Scientifically and magically. He was willing to use any means to his ends."

Michael's face remained bland.

Rudy shifted in his seat, typing a little slower. Out of the corner of my eye, I saw him glance quickly at me.

I started to get a bad feeling. "You mentioned your former witch had more than one leashed shifter. How many did he have?" I asked Michael.

"Four."

I gaped. "Four? That's impossible."

He started typing, his face eerily blue by the light of the laptop. "I assure you, it's true."

"How come no one knew?"

"It was a secret he killed to guard."

I looked at Rudy. "Were you one of his shifters?"

He kept his eyes on his own computer screen. He licked his bottom lip and shook his head. "Not leashed, no."

I waited, but he said nothing else. Nor did he look at me. Oddly quiet, for Rudy.

"Are you from Brazil, too?"

"Nope. I'm a Florida boy." He tried to grin, but it was strained.

"How'd you meet Michael?" This was as forthcoming with information about their past as either of them had been since I'd met them. While I was understandably curious about them, I wasn't so sure I was going to be happy with what I found out.

Rudy finally stopped typing and glanced at Michael.

The cat looked up and gave a small shrug. "She might as well know now."

"All of it?"

Michael turned back to his laptop. "She's got a right to know."

Okay. Now I was scared. It was Michael who'd always dodged the issue or flat-out refused to talk when I'd asked about their past. Was he being open now just because of our situation?

Probably.

But, again, that didn't mean I'd like it.

Rudy bit his lip. He glanced at me, those crystal-blue eyes weighted with doubt. Finally he grimaced. Sitting back, he typed one last sequence on his keyboard, then faced me. "I met Michael in Brazil. I was…one of Alessandro's playthings."

"Huh? Playthings?"

He sighed, combing a hand through his hair. "A prostitute. He bought me and kept me as a pet."

My fork clattered to my mostly empty plate. I stared at Rudy, trying to comprehend what he'd revealed. "You're kidding."

He watched my fork settle, pushing a breath through his lips. "Nope."

"Wow."

He laughed. "I'm not sure how to take that response."

Neither was I. I shook my head. "Whoa."

"He didn't learn all those sex tricks from me."

We both turned to look at Michael, who continued to type without looking up.

"But…" I glanced at Rudy. "If you…*belonged* to Alessandro, then how did the two of you get together?"

Rudy sighed. "How much do you know about BDSM?"

My blood started to chill. "I know what it is."

He nodded. "Well, that was my relationship with Alessandro. Heavy on the sadomasochism. One night, things got a bit…um, rough, and he almost killed me. I was dying anyway, so he brought Michael to me and told him to change me."

"You weren't a wolf yet?"

"Not yet."

Which meant he'd been a fully human pet without any added benefit of being a shifter. I shivered.

"Michael was my savior. Alessandro gave me to him and basically told him to either bring me back to life or get rid of the body."

It made a kind of warped sense. Quite often infecting people cured them of diseases or other life-threatening ailments. Trouble was, the cure was often worse than the disease. You pretty much had to bleed out and be infected by a shifter. The infection happened when the shifter's blood got into the wounded human's system. If they were very lucky, whatever was unique about shifter blood traveled into the victim's blood and caused the change. When analyzed through scientific means, a shifter's blood didn't look any different than a mundane person's blood, but there was an indefinable trace of magic that created the difference. It was that magic that only another shifter or a witch could detect. The change was rapid. The blood supply would beef up and new healing blood targeted the fatal wound. Even then, the person didn't always live. And if they did, that wasn't the end of it. Some people just couldn't handle the change. The magic interacted with their brain chemistry and didn't mix well. They either had something like epileptic seizures that killed them, or they went completely berserk and had to be destroyed. Usually done by another shifter, any kind of shifter. It was something inside the person that decided what animal they became, not the shifter that "sired" them, like in most books and movies. So becoming a shifter wasn't something most people chose to do.

Rudy went on. "I lived, but it took a while. Michael nursed me back to health. How could I not fall in love?"

Michael snorted.

I chewed my bottom lip. "You said before that you and Michael have been together a little over a year, but that you chased him for two."

"Yeah."

"How long were you with Alessandro before…the incident?"

"Just about a year."

I let that hang. Rudy was only twenty now. That would make him…too young for what he'd lived through. No wonder I often saw far more experience in his eyes than belonged there for his age.

The room got quiet. I didn't know what to say or where to look. That was quite a bomb to drop on me. Rudy had been a prostitute of the far-too-young variety? Rudy had been *owned* by another person? Leashing was one thing. It was a magical bond between witch and shifter. But owning someone like that, just for the sake of pleasure? I'd known such things occurred, of course, but I'd never met anyone actually involved. At least, not to my knowledge. Although, if you ask me, the owning part wasn't too far off the mark from what Roland had intended for me.

I jumped to feel Rudy's hand slide over mine where it rested on the table. I looked up into earnest blue eyes. "We're still okay, right, Meg?"

I turned my hand over and squeezed his fingers. That wasn't enough. I pushed myself from my chair and into his lap, wrapping my arms around his neck. This was *Rudy.* He'd managed to crawl into my heart in the last few days, and he stayed there, whatever his past. "We're okay. I…Wow, that's quite a past, but I don't think any less of you or anything."

He hugged me fiercely, and I understood his personal worry, at least, in revealing his past.

I swiped at the tear that dribbled down my cheek and sat back in his lap. The towel had fallen open, and I swatted at his playfully wandering hands. "Stop that." I twisted so I could see Michael, trying to pull the towel up. "But that doesn't explain why Shannon was so hot for you. She's not all that interested in science."

One of Michael's muscular shoulders lifted and dropped in a blasé shrug. "She must have heard the rumors."

"What rumors?"

"That Alessandro had a shifter who was born a witch."

I frowned. "That's imposs... Oh, come on!"

He raised those gorgeous green eyes to stare steadily at me.

I gaped. "No way!"

He sighed and finally put aside the laptop, setting it open on the mattress beside him. "Alessandro was trying to develop a serum to shift a person without the usual trauma. He'd gather young children off the streets as guinea pigs. I was one of them. None of us knew I was gifted until they'd already started infecting me."

"Started infecting you?"

He nodded. "That's what they called it. The serum worked almost a third of the time, and sometimes the side effects were livable. But the individual had to be young—around puberty was best—and the process of infection took multiple injections over the space of about three years. I was over a year into the process when my gifts were discovered."

I couldn't shut my mouth or make my bugged-out eyes go back to normal.

"There were a few months where I could almost work magic, but by the time the three years were up, I was a shifter with no magic."

"Why didn't they stop the infection process?"

"I would have died. Once the process started, if it stopped, the subject died."

"This happened when you were a kid?"

He nodded. "I was thirteen when the process started."

"And you're thirty-two now?"

Another nod.

"You were his shifter for that long?"

"He didn't leash me until my twenties. I was kept at the dormitory before that."

"Dormitory?"

"Basically it was a fortified ranch where he kept us. We were guarded heavily, but the grounds were quite extensive, so it didn't feel so much like prison."

"Goddess!"

He shrugged. "As prisons go, it was a relatively nice one. I had all I asked for, except anything that would allow me unsupervised communication with the outside world."

"What happened in your twenties?"

"He decided to try leashing me and a few of the others."

"Were the others witches, too?"

"Only one. The other gifted children who were infected died."

He was an anomaly. A frickin' miracle!

He watched me. Waiting. I didn't have a clue what to say. And I'd thought that Rudy's past was a bomb!

"What happened? If you were leashed, when Alessandro died, you would have died."

"True. If he had died in the explosion as everyone has been told."

"He didn't?"

"No. He was dead before the explosion."

I was afraid to ask. "What happened?"

"He tried something profoundly stupid which weakened our leashes enough for us to free ourselves."

"What did he do?"

Michael's eyes met Rudy's. "He tried to leash another."

"Rudy?"

"Yes."

"Why?"

Rudy hugged me closer. "To make sure I stayed around. To make sure that Michael stayed around."

"Alessandro found out that we were in love. He was afraid that Rudy would attempt to leave because of what had happened between them. He decided if he leashed him, it would prevent that."

My head reeled. I reached up to rub the bridge of my nose. "So he tried to leash Rudy, it weakened the other leashes, and you broke free. How'd he die?"

"We killed him."

"'We'?"

"The four of us. His leashed shifters."

"He was that bad, huh?"

"As masters go, he was a relatively good one. He saw to it that we had everything we wanted. Except our freedom, of course. I learned quite a bit during my time with him."

Nearly twenty years of captivity. It was mind-blowing to think about.

"But what he did was wrong. He planned to create an army of shifters, and we couldn't allow that." Michael sat back against the massive black headboard, crossing his arms over his bare chest. "So, I can only guess that Shannon heard the rumors of what Alessandro had been doing in his labs. From what I gather, most of the grand leaders have heard the rumors by now. I've gotten a number of invitations from around the world."

His frank gaze told me all. "But that's just trading one prison for another."

He nodded.

I grimaced. "No wonder you were pissed off when I leashed you."

A tight, rueful grin spread across his lips. "Yes. But your prison has proven to have certain benefits."

I stared at him, heart pounding. "I offered to let you go."

The grin evaporated. "Yes. Repeatedly. I wonder if you want to keep me at all." His words twisted even though his expression was bland. "Especially now that you know what I am. You don't seem to like unusual situations, after all. And I would certainly qualify as 'unusual.'"

I couldn't argue any of that. I'd known he was unusual almost from the start, and he just kept proving the point. I stood, clutching my towel around my torso as I walked away from Rudy despite his tug on my hand as I started across the room. "So that's why you know so much about magic."

"Yes."

Rudy half stood from his chair.

"Sit down," Michael snapped.

Standing, Rudy faced him. "But—"

"Sit."

The chair creaked as Rudy's weight settled on it. He crossed his arms over his chest, an unhappy frown on his normally smiling face.

I swallowed. Okay. I got it. I'd had my moment with Rudy. This was between Michael and me. We had to hash it out. Damn it. I propped my butt up against the edge of a solid oak dresser that stood not far from the foot of the bed. I watched my hands as I toyed with the edges of the towel wrapped around me. "Can you still feel it?"

"What?"

"Magic."

"Yes."

"But you can't use it."

His pause was long enough that I chanced a look at him. Those green eyes watched me steadily. "No."

"I'm sorry."

"Don't be. I imagine it's like being a sensitive." There were many, many people sensitive to magic in the world, but only a select few who could manipulate it.

"Still. You're quite a catch. I can see why Shannon would want you." I braced myself and looked up at him. "Why don't you want her?"

His eyes narrowed, but he said nothing.

So I continued. "She's the grand dame of the Southwest. You deserve to belong to a witch with power like that."

"That's a different kind of power." He turned and clicked his laptop shut. "Magically speaking, she's not powerful enough to hold me."

I blinked, watching him as he edged to the side of the bed. "What? You think you could break her leash?"

"Eventually, yes, I think I could."

"Then you could probably break mine."

"But I don't *want* to break yours. There's a difference."

I frowned, not sure if I should be flattered or scared by that.

"Besides, you've bested her. That makes you the more powerful witch."

"That was a long time ago. She's probably gained in power since then."

"Mostly likely." He placed the computer on the nightstand and stood. The open red shirt framed mouth-watering pecs and abs, but I told myself not to notice. Yeah, like that ever worked. "But then again, so have you. After all, you're holding the power of two witches, and you've managed to leash two shifters where she hasn't managed to leash one."

I snugged my arms more securely under my breasts, too aware of my perky nipples for this conversation. *This is serious!* I told them. "I'm sure that's by choice."

"Is it?"

Good question. Was it? "Why would you want me to keep you?"

He crossed his arms and leaned a shoulder against one of the sturdy end posts of the bed. Silky black hair edged down over his right eye, almost hiding it. "I can think of a number of reasons. Chief among them that I'm not likely going to be allowed to live unleashed for any length of time.

I'm shocked I lasted as long as I did after Alessandro's death. If the grand leaders have suspicions about what I am, one of them will force the issue eventually."

"Did Shannon already try that?"

"She requested, but she didn't cast the guardian spell. I believe she was being polite and waiting for me to come to her."

I nodded. "But I got in the way."

"Obviously."

"Politically speaking, she's got all sorts of contacts."

He shook his head. "*She* has contacts. Those same contacts wouldn't necessarily be mine. Besides, I have my own contacts."

I gnawed at the side of my thumbnail. "So you're just as happy with a witch who has no connections."

"For now."

"'For now'? What does that mean?" I pointed my finger at him when he didn't answer. "I don't want power and politics, Michael. If I did, I'd have stayed with my mother."

He pushed from the bedpost and stepped toward me. I knew that heated look in those hooded eyes, and it made my belly go liquid. "So you've said."

I tried not to shiver at the sound of that low rumble. "I'm serious."

"I believe you." He stopped a step before me, invading my space with all that feline masculine virility. Goddess, I wouldn't blame Shannon for wanting him just for that. "But the case remains that here we are. You're under suspicion for a magical murder that you *did* commit. You're currently holding the power of two witches. You're holding the leashes of two shifters. And, I might add, they're not normal leashes."

I saw Rudy move out of the corner of my eye, but I couldn't take my gaze off Michael to see what he was doing. "What?"

Michael shook his head, leaning toward me. He didn't touch me, but by bracing those big hands on the edge of the dresser to either side of my hips, he surrounded me with heat and that deep, dark scent of his that made my skin tingle. "Whatever it was that the three of us did to accommodate Roland's power, it's made the leashes more than what they should be. Can't you feel it?"

"I've never leashed anyone before. You know that."

He leaned in and touched just his lips to the tingling skin over my heart. "I have been leashed, and I can tell you that I'm much more tightly tied to you than I ever was to Alessandro. His leashes stayed firmly in hand, where yours have moved to the heart."

"I thought…" I breathed him in, nose hovering over the glossy black of his hair. "I thought that was how leashes worked."

"They form a bond, yes," he whispered against my skin. "But not like ours."

I swallowed. "It's the sex."

He shook his head, lips brushing my collarbone. "I had sex with Alessandro. That's not it."

Why it surprised me to hear that he'd had sex with his former witch, I don't know. I'd seen him with Rudy plenty, enough to know that he was most definitely bisexual. I guess I just hadn't considered him with anyone other than Rudy.

I let my head fall back, blinking at the ceiling. Trying to think despite the sensual haze he was settling around me. "So where does that leave us?"

His hands slid up my arms, raising goosebumps. One dug into the hair at the back of my skull; the other ended spanned over my back, supporting my weight as he stepped into me. "Exactly where we were." I lowered my eyes to a face of masculine lines and feline curves. He kissed me briefly, lips only. "Trying to figure out how to get you out of this alive. Everything else will have to wait."

My hands clutched his biceps. The tuck of my towel gave. "Wait. We should talk about this." His kiss hushed me briefly, but I kept talking afterward. "We can't answer everything with sex."

"Oh, but we can." He turned, taking me with him.

I stumbled in his embrace, forced to walk backward as he aimed me toward the bed.

"Our connection is through sex," he continued as we went. "Our bond strengthens through sex. It may be that through sex we can find a way to disguise what you did."

He stopped when the backs of my legs hit the edge of the mattress.

Another pair of hands tugged the towel from my back. Rudy's lips closed on a healing bite wound on my shoulder as he spirited the towel away, leaving me naked between them.

"Do you really think that?" I asked Michael as he released me into Rudy's arms.

Michael smiled as he eased out of the red shirt. "It's our best chance."

Rudy turned my face to his, involving me in a kiss so I didn't get to watch Michael shuck his jeans. I couldn't complain, though. The wolf pressed my back to his chest, one hand cupping my head while the other slid from my belly down to the juncture of my thighs. Knowing fingers pressed in and found the pooling moisture waiting there. I groaned, settling down and spreading my legs to allow him better access. He sank to his knees, leaning back slightly. His cock, long and hard, poked my back.

My neck started hurting, so I broke from the kiss, facing forward again. Rudy's lips trailed down my neck back to the bite mark on my shoulder.

Michael stood, naked and wonderfully aroused, at the edge of the bed, caressing his erection as he watched Rudy's fingers dip inside me and swirl around my clit. He knelt on the floor and put his big hands on the insides of my thighs, pressing them further apart. Rudy's fingers tapped on my clit, teasing me. Michael leaned in and traced a long, wet line with his tongue on the bend between my crotch and leg.

I moaned.

Rudy adjusted us again so that he was now sitting flush, my butt pressed to the inside of his thighs. His cock pressed against my spine.

Michael pushed my legs up higher, lapping at the back of one knee before he settled on his belly.

Rudy's fingers splayed open my soaked sex, exposing it to Michael.

The cat leaned in and traced both fingers and sex with his tongue, a light touch, teasing. I growled, pushing against their hands, trying to make Michael do something serious. But he held me still and continued to lightly, almost delicately, lap at me.

Rudy's fingers massaged me just outside the lips of my sex, rubbing my juices everywhere except where I was most sensitive.

I finally remembered my hands and plunged them into the cool silk of Michael's hair, pushing his face where I wanted it. "Suck."

I felt his chuckle as his mouth opened. That tongue finally took a hard, long swipe at my sex, and my entire body shuddered in thanks.

Rudy's wet fingers slid up my body to find one of my nipples, and I reached up to pluck the other nipple myself. But my main focus was on the mouth feasting on me, sucking hard to plump me up.

"Oh, Goddess, someone please fuck me."

With a loud, sucking pop, Michael lifted his head. He surged up to kneel on the bed between my thighs. But instead of plunging in as I'd hoped, he leaned forward to put both hands under my arms and lift me.

"Ride Rudy," he told me.

I glanced down. Rudy had fallen onto his back, and his wonderful long cock was red, hard, and more than ready for me. Eagerly I used Michael for balance with one hand, then used the other to grab Rudy, pump him once, then sink down. We both groaned at the bliss of it. I had to be careful because of his length, but Michael solved that problem by urging me farther onto my back. We hadn't tried this yet. Rudy put his hands on my hips to guide me, steady me, and I leaned back on my arms for balance. Michael urged my knees farther up toward Rudy's hips. Both his hands and Rudy's guided my hips in small circles, which did marvelous things to the hard friction of that rod within my wet cunt. Rudy waited until I got a rhythm going, then started to rock his hips. He bent his knees up to either side of Michael's hips, and that gave him a bit more leverage to pump into me.

"Oh, man, why haven't we done this before?" I groaned.

Michael grinned. "It gets better."

I watched, wide-eyed, as he lowered his head again.

"Goddess!" I cried, watching his tongue start low on Rudy's cock and swipe up until the tip circled my clit. Cunt stretched by the cock filling me, my clit was far more sensitive than usual. I felt the need to squirm, but the position didn't allow it.

But movement by me didn't seem to be necessary. Rudy continued to rock, fucking me slowly from underneath, while Michael sampled us both.

See, that just plain did it for me. Michael's lips sucked in my clit, and then his tongue slid down off my sex and onto Rudy's. I looked down and saw his hand working, which meant he was either fondling Rudy's scrumptious, furry balls, or he was fingering Rudy's tight little ass. Just the thought sent me off and I came in a guttering moan, writhing as best I could while my body shook.

"Mmmm." Michael glanced up at me, the lower half of his face glistening. "Did you like that?"

I nodded, biting my lip.

Michael used his free hand to smack the outside of Rudy's hip. "Faster, wolf."

Rudy slammed up into me, and I cried out, shoved just that easily back onto the brink of vicious pleasure. Michael left the bed, but I was too busy getting fucked to track his movements. Rudy's fingers dug into my hips, and my breasts jolted with the force of his thrusts. I groaned, clutching the sheets underneath him for dear life.

Michael had gone to get lube. He knelt between Rudy's thighs, slathering clear liquid over that huge cock of his.

I opened my eyes wide. "You can't both fit!" I managed to gasp.

He grinned. "This isn't for you this time."

My jaw dropped, and twin groans came from both my and Rudy's throats. Rudy's pumping stopped by necessity as Michael grasped his thighs. He dragged Rudy's ass up toward his crotch, lifting both of us. I hissed when the new angle thudded the crown of Rudy's cock at my cervix. Michael positioned his cock down below my sex and pushed in. Rudy's moan was pure, agonizing joy.

Michael leaned in, reaching down to grip Rudy's waist. The insides of his forearms brushed my hips, muscles bunching as he impaled Rudy. He rocked in, and Rudy just about died underneath me, moaning. A glance down showed me claws where his human form should have had nails, gouging out the heavy duvet.

"Open up, Meg," Michael crooned, leaning in to brush the tips of my jouncing breasts with his tongue. "Open the leashes."

At mention of them, my control on the leashes dissolved and the links between us burst wide open. I trembled and collapsed back on Rudy's chest, awash in the heated, brutal pleasure that gripped my wolf. Our wolf. Michael fucked him with lazy precision, rubbing that spot that drove him wild. But Rudy managed to hold it. He managed to not come, drawing strength and control from me. From Michael. Using us to prop up his own shattering control as agonizing pleasure seared through his veins.

"This is us, Meg," Michael rasped, leaning in so that his belly pressed against my clit. Delicious pressure from without to match the painfully beautiful pressure from within.

I gritted my teeth over a scream, my own control fraying rapidly at the edges.

Michael's iron will started to melt and his hips slammed into Rudy with ruthless abandon. "This is us."

Power welled up, lava hot, searing me from within. This time I did cry out as I erupted. Heat shot through the leashes, slamming into both of my lovers. We couldn't hope for control and could only hang on, clutching each other as the pleasure-power spread over us.

Chapter Ten

The knock woke us.

I cracked my eye, glaring at the door over the sparsely furry expanse of Michael's chest. I wanted to yell "go away," but my throat wouldn't work.

The knock sounded again.

"What is it?" Michael yelled.

After a moment, the knock sounded again.

I patted his chest and managed to croak, "They can't hear. The sealing."

"Tch!" Groaning, he rolled out from under me, then off the edge of the bed.

Rudy's weight, sprawled across my back, pushed me into the mattress as I watched Michael grab his jeans from the floor. He put them on, not bothering to button them all the way before yanking the door open. I removed the sealing spell from the area around the door.

"What is it?"

A man—a shifter—was on the other side. He was probably around my age, with dark brown curls cropped short around a square face. Brown eyes widened at the sight of Michael. A sniff, probably involuntary, preceded a quick glance toward the bed, where he saw me, tousled, nakedness hidden under an equally naked Rudy.

"Uh…" He tried to recover, stepping back a pace into the hallway. "Ms. Cavanagh is downstairs and would like to speak to Ms. Grey."

"Now?" Michael demanded.

"Yes."

"What time is it?" I croaked.

He glanced at me and had the good sense to blush. "Eleven o'clock," he said, averting his eyes.

I shoved up partially on my elbows. "No way!"

"She'll be down after she takes a shower," Michael told him.

"Uh, but she said come now."

"Tell the grand dame what you saw. Tell her we just got up. I'm sure she'll appreciate the shower."

"Uh, yeah. Right. I'll tell her."

Michael shut the door.

"Well, nothing like rubbing her nose in it," I mused, folding my arms beneath my chin. I raised the sealing spell again, trying not to dwell on just how in tune I was to it.

Rudy sighed, sliding a hand down my side and nuzzling the back of my neck. After our explosive encounter last night, we'd all collapsed in an exhausted heap. Even Michael hadn't managed our normal clean up. So we were all quite fragrant and quite sticky. It was kind of disgusting, but in a warm, fuzzy sort of way.

We took turns showering, turns that overlapped. We very nearly had sex again but decided that it wouldn't be prudent to leave Shannon waiting *that* long.

I pulled my wet hair back into a ponytail as Michael and Rudy finished dressing. Camo khakis for Rudy with an army-green T-shirt. Jeans and a black button-down— buttoned this time—for Michael. Blue, long-sleeved polo and jeans for me. You'd think it was just a normal day.

We trooped into the hallway and Michael stopped me briefly. "Lock it," he advised, glancing at the door.

I glanced at the doorknob, then realized he meant magically. "Good idea." With a thought, I activated another spell that locked the door.

Another of Shannon's shifters was stationed at the end of the hall, seated on a chair just above the sweeping staircase that led down to the main hall. He looked up from his Game Boy, but didn't stop us. I rolled my eyes when I saw him touch a Bluetooth receiver in his ear. How very secret service.

"They know we're coming?" I asked, stopping before him with a smart grin on my lips.

He matched it. "Yep." He was kinda cute, with short, dark brown hair and shining hazel eyes in a foxy, triangular face. I was quite sure he looked younger than he had to be.

"Fine. Wanna tell me where they are so I don't have to search the house?"

"Dining room."

"Thanks."

"Don't mention it."

We got to the dining room to find Shannon seated to the right of the end of the table nearest the French doors that led outside. A breeze beyond the beveled glass stirred the branches of the trees that lined the paved walkway leading from the house, brushing their branches against the doors. Shannon stared at them, blonde perfection in the mottled sunlight. Three of her shifters lined the wall behind her, all dressed in casual bodyguard chic.

The blue eyes Shannon turned to me showed disdain. "Meg. Sorry to have wakened you. I didn't expect you'd sleep in so late."

I grinned a bit too brightly perhaps. "We had a busy night last night."

She glanced at the two shifters behind me and grimaced. "Yes. I see." She waved at her own men and pointed at the French doors. "I would like to speak to you privately. Your shifters may wait with mine outside."

I glanced back at Michael and Rudy. Michael hesitated, then shrugged. He brushed a fond hand over the curve of my jaw before following Shannon's shifters to the door. Rudy grinned at me, kissed his fingertips, touched them to my lips, then followed Michael.

I had to smile and still wore it when the door clicked shut behind them. They all stood where they could see us, still guarding their respective charges. Truthfully, there might not be much they could do against a witch on her guard, but they were doing their jobs nonetheless.

Shannon waved a hand, and I felt her sealing spell settling in on the room, no doubt soundproofing it. "My, you've changed." Her look was coolly speculative.

I rested my hands on the back of the chair across from her. "Have I?"

"You have. The Meg I knew wouldn't have dreamed of leashing anyone. I seem to recall you saying that no one had the right to own anyone else."

"I don't own them."

"You don't."

"I've leashed them, yes, but it's not what you think."

"It isn't?"

"No." Why was I telling her this? Trying to make someone I'd once wanted as a friend understand? "I called them, but I was willing to let them go if they didn't want to help me."

Shannon frowned. "Even with the threat of Roland Parks?"

"Even then."

"And they stayed."

"They did."

"So the bond between you is mutual, then. How touching. And you've known each other, what? A week?"

"About that, yeah." I sighed. Trying to explain things to Shannon always had been hopeless. She and I just didn't think the same. "What do you want, Shannon?"

She waved a ringed hand at the chair I held. "Have a seat. We have something to discuss."

What the hell. I sat. "We do?"

"Yes." She folded her hands primly on the polished wood before her. "There are serious charges leveled against you."

I folded my arms on the table and leaned forward a bit. "I'm aware of that."

"I'm willing to help you."

"You are?"

"In exchange for Miguel Sandoval."

"Michael."

"Excuse me?"

"His name's Michael."

"You are aware that he's from Brazil."

"I'm aware of that, yes. But his name's Michael." If it was Miguel, he'd have told me. I was pretty sure of that.

She waved a hand in the air, brushing the issue aside. "Fine. Michael Sandoval is too much shifter for you. I'm sure you've realized that."

"I know he's quite a shifter."

"And he's worthy of a grand dame."

"That he is."

"So. Hand over his leash to me, and I will help you out of your little dilemma."

Whoa! Was she serious? "How?"

"How what?"

"How will you help me?"

"Do we have a deal?"

"How will you help me?"

"Meg."

"Shannon."

She spread her hands flat on the table. "The only evidence against you is the testimony of the witches and shifters who saw what happened on Samhain. Amateur, fledgling witches and unleashed shifters."

I nodded. "Neither are known to be very reliable eye-witnesses for magic."

"My opinion as grand dame on this matter holds quite a bit of weight. More so because I knew Roland Parks."

My eyes narrowed. She did? "How well did you know Roland?"

"Well enough."

I stared at her coolly composed face for a very long, very thoughtful moment. A bunch of wonderings scampered across my brain, chief among them a wonder why memories of Shannon failed to surface. "Shannon…did you tell Roland about me?"

She didn't even blink. "Tell him what about you?"

"Did you tell him who I am? My family?"

One blonde brow rose slightly. I think one side of her mouth twitched. "I might have mentioned it."

I slapped my hands on the table, leaning in. Out of the corner of my eye, I saw all the shifters outside tense, but none of them tried to come inside. Neither did Shannon bat an eye. "You bitch! Did you know what he had in mind for me?!" I didn't dare search the memories now, and no recollection of Roland and Shannon ever meeting sprang to mind.

"Of course I didn't. If I had, I would have put a stop to it."

"Easy enough to say now."

"Are you accusing me of something, Meg?"

I took a deep breath and forced myself to sit back. "No."

She nodded. "Good. If you had come to me a long time ago, I could have put a stop to all of this."

I didn't believe her. I couldn't believe her.

"Instead, you tried to handle this all on your own and blundered. And now a man is dead. I'm *trying* to help you, Meg."

"I still don't see what you can do."

"If you had my backing when the tribunal arrives, it would go a long way toward proving you innocent. Especially as everyone is aware of our past."

It was true. Shannon speaking on my behalf would be remarkable to anyone who knew even a little bit about our history. "And you'd do that. For me."

She nodded. "In exchange for Michael Sandoval."

"What about Rudy?"

"The wolf? You can keep him."

I grinned a nasty grin. "Shannon, you haven't been paying attention, have you? They're a couple."

She frowned, clueless.

I was happy to help her out. "They're in love. They're lovers. They're not going to want to be separated."

"But they're with you."

I put on my best imitation of Rudy's wolfish grin. "Yeah."

She blinked and I almost laughed. How the heck could you be the grand dame of the Southwest and be blind to a homosexual couple? I mean, hello! San Francisco was in her jurisdiction.

She sat back, trying to recover. "I hadn't realized. *Senhor* Sandoval and I didn't get very far in our discussions when we first met."

I waited for her to think. She'd have to know that she couldn't take one without the other. Yes, leashed shifters had relationships, but rarely could two shifters leashed to two different witches maintain any kind of close bond. There were too many conflicting responsibilities.

While I waited, I did some thinking of my own. She was right, after all. I would be put to death if they found me guilty of murdering Roland with magic. My biggest concern there was that I *was* guilty. Yes, there were mitigating circumstances, but I'd still done it. Was it worth keeping Michael and Rudy to chance death? After all, we'd only known each other about a week. True, a lot had happened in those few days, but it just wasn't a lot of time. We could very well regret linking ourselves if I survived this. They could finally realize what a boring little nothing I really was and not want me around. Wouldn't it be better to make a clean break now? They'd hold an honored place with Shannon. At least Michael would, and he'd see after Rudy. When you looked at it plain and simple like that, I really should take her offer.

She took a breath and looked back up at me, calmly composed again. "The fact remains that I want Michael Sandoval. I'll take them both."

"Just like that."

She grimaced. "Meg, you're not in much of a position to bargain."

True. "Do you think you can leash them both?" Yeah. I was buying time.

Her brows crouched in on her slightly narrowed eyes. "That's not the point."

"But it is. You think if I hand over Michael that Rudy will just trot along blithely behind him?"

The glossy peach lipstick got hidden when she pressed her lips together in a grimace.

I stared at her face and realization hit me. I couldn't do it. They didn't belong with this cold woman. She didn't have enough...oh, what? Imagination? Color? Personality for them. "You think Michael will let me hand him over at all?" I shook my head, laughing tightly. "You *really* don't know him. You've got to hold them tight and hold them both, or it doesn't work, Shannon."

"You are not that much more powerful than I."

Wow. Déjà vu. We'd had tons of exchanges like this as kids. Despite all the evidence, she never willingly believed that I had way more juice than she did. I cocked my head to the side. "I'm not? Then how come I've got two shifters and you don't have any?"

She shot to her feet, surprising me and, by the looks of it, her shifters. "I'm the grand dame of the Southwest," she hissed, the calm façade crumbling to reveal the spiteful teenager I used to know so well. "I was judged powerful enough to hold a sixth of the United States, I think I can handle two shifters."

"Why don't you have a shifter already, Shannon? Most grand leaders do."

"That is not your concern."

"Can you even hold a single shifter, Shannon?"

"You bitch! How dare you question my abilities? Of *course* I can hold a shifter!"

"Well, you can't have mine."

"Stupid! You could never see a good offer when it came to you. I don't know why I even bothered."

"Neither do I."

She motioned to the men outside, and her shifters led the way through the French doors. The three of them ranged behind her while Michael and Rudy stood behind my chair. By the time everyone had stopped moving, Shannon's calm was firmly back in place.

Shannon eyed Michael hungrily through that mask. I thought she might bring up the subject directly, but I was wrong. "The tribunal will be here in three days. Marie

Mercier of the Mid-South, Sandra Mendez of Central Mexico, and Jack Kamski of Eastern Canada will all be in attendance."

Damn! Actual grand leaders were coming to see about little ol' me?

Shannon glowered at me, as yet unable to regain her cool. "Your mother is also sending a representative." She smiled, nasty-like. "Julian Newland."

I blinked, gaping. "My father?"

She nodded and looked satisfied to have caught me off guard. "You will stay on the premises until they arrive."

With that, she was done with me. She turned and led her shifters out the open arch into the main hallway, dispelling her sealing spell on the way out. I saw Aggie and Hannah catch up to her in the hall, but didn't bother to wonder about them. I stayed seated, staring at the huge arrangement of gardenias in the middle of the table.

The chair beside me scraped back and Michael sat down. Rudy's hand squeezed my shoulder on the other side.

Neither of them said anything, just waited.

I finally shook my head. "My father. Terrific."

"Bad news?" Rudy asked.

"No. Just…damn. What does he want to get mixed up in this for?"

"He's your father," Michael pointed out.

I smiled. "He was more of a sperm donor than anything. I only knew him distantly as I grew up. Their deal was that I belonged to my mother. She made the same deal with all our fathers."

"Do any of you have the same father?" Rudy asked.

"Nope. The closest I got to a father was Talia's dad. She's the oldest. Richard's as close to a husband as Mom ever allowed, and that's only because he lets her rule him." I bowed my head, pressing at the corners of my eyes with thumb and forefinger. "Goddess. I guess it's time I called my mother." I stood. "But could we get something to eat first? I'm starved."

I glanced toward the main hall to find it empty. Shannon must have left.

We stepped through the door that led from the dining room to the kitchen. We took Deidre by surprise by the looks of it. The small woman stood at a free-standing butcher's block, chopping vegetables. Her long brown hair was pulled back in a simple tail, displaying the plain features of her round face. If you asked me, her eyes were her best feature. Huge and brown, with heavy lids and long black lashes.

She blinked, eyeing the men at my back. She sent another glance toward the small four-seater in the breakfast nook, where two shifters sat drinking coffee and reading the paper. They eyed us, then exchanged glances.

Ignoring them, I pulled myself onto one of the barstools that lined one side of the counter, where the range and the sink resided. The kitchen was laid out perfectly for one of those cooking shows on the Food Channel. I smiled sweetly at Deidre. The kitchen was her domain, and it paid to be nice to a person on their home turf. "Think we could get something to eat?"

She glanced at the veggies she was chopping. "I was getting ready for tonight's dinner, but there's some batter left from the pancakes this morning."

"I'll do it," Rudy volunteered, rounding to her side of the counter. He blinked prettily at her. "If you don't mind."

I laughed at her look of surprise. "Don't let him fool you. He looks like a worthless teenager, but he's really quite handy in the kitchen."

"Hey!" he groused, mock glaring at me.

I batted my eyelashes at him. "And a fabulous cook to boot."

In no time, Rudy had Deidre at ease and back to her veggies while he fixed pancakes for the three of us. He asked her what she was making, then proceeded to discuss the recipe with her as he cooked.

Not long after Rudy started setting things out for himself, one of the shifters from the table approached Michael.

"Mr. Sandoval?"

Michael turned on his barstool to face him. "Yes?"

The shifter, a shortish, roundish wolf by the look of him, extended his hand. "Jake Tearney. District Attorney Cook said I should introduce myself when I got the chance."

Michael's eyebrows rose in surprise, and he took the man's hand. "You work for Howard?"

"No. I work for Larry Peters."

Michael nodded and smiled. "Ah. I met Larry last week. How did you get assigned here?"

"The grand dame asked for reinforcements. Cook says it's necessary before a tribunal." The man glanced at me, dark blue eyes wary. "We're impartial, you understand, but Howard wanted you to know we were here."

"Thank you," Michael spoke for us. "And thank Howard."

They smiled and exchanged pleasantries. I made a note to ask who this Larry Peters guy was, but if he worked for Howard Cook, then these guys might just be a bit more on our side. I took a second look at them both. They had the look of cops or marines about them. But then, if they were shifter enforcers, the marine look made sense.

Everything was going fine and I could almost forget the tenuous situation we were in, but then Aggie and Hannah ruined it. Bitch One and Bitch Two stormed imperiously through the door when I was almost done with my stack of pancakes.

Aggie waited for me to meet her gaze. "We must discuss the coven."

I raised a brow, my fork hovering over cake, butter, and syrup that I very much wished to finish. "We must?"

"That *is*, after all, what you originally came here to discuss."

"It is?" I carefully cut another bite. "Funny. I thought you brought me here so Shannon could trap me and you could accuse me of murder."

"You *did* kill Roland," Hannah spat.

Aggie held up a hand, halting her words. "Perhaps we acted rashly."

"Oh?" Okay, that was interesting. I put my fork down and gave them my full attention, swallowing what was already in my mouth.

Aggie looked to the shifters who were again sitting quietly at the breakfast table. "Perhaps we should go somewhere to discuss this privately."

I eyed my breakfast and sighed. "Okay, maybe we should." I glanced at Michael, who nodded. He'd already finished. Stubbornly, I took one last bite before climbing off my stool. "Rudy, you can stay and eat if you want." After all, he'd just started in on his own stack of pancakes.

He glanced from me to Michael and back. "You sure?"

Michael stood. "I'll go with her. You eat."

"Okay."

Aggie turned to Deidre. "Deidre, go get Chloe and Melissa, and meet us in the game room."

Deidre forlornly eyed her vegetables.

"I'll finish them if you like," Rudy offered.

"You don't mind?"

"Nah. You go ahead. I'll start that sauce that we talked about."

She gave him a genuine smile that lit up her face. As I said, the way to Deidre's heart was through food. "Thank you." She wiped her hands on the towel she had tucked into her waistband. Her smile was gone and her eyes were fearful when she looked up at Aggie. "I'll get Chloe and Melissa." She left the towel on the butcher's block and fled.

A dozen of Roland's memories sped across my mind as we followed Aggie and Hannah out of the room. I don't think Roland had even noted the animosity within his coven. I don't think he cared. Especially since all of them were too weak to do much about anything.

The game room. Yeah, sure. Yes, to anyone who didn't know, it did look like a pretty cool basement that served as an adult play room. There was a fancy mahogany game table that sat in the middle of the room, with six matching carved chairs. In one corner were two mint-condition arcade games, a darts game, and a Pachinko. Along the last wall was an entertainment center with a nice sofa set arranged before it. But Roland had never used this room for those types of games. Not regularly. However, if you moved the game table and the expensive Oriental rug beneath it, you'd see the circle of power etched there. It was one of the two permanent circles at the house; the other was located outside by the pool. The bricks that fashioned the floor were specially made, pure earth with a hard resin to seal the top. The pure earth was excellent for conducting spells. Fancy candle sconces alternated with electric lights along the walls since you didn't want to have electricity running when you were circling. A breaker box hidden behind the bar beside the sofa cut the power to the entire room with one switch.

But I wasn't supposed to know any of that, so I struggled not to show it in my face. Michael and I took seats at the barstools beside the bar. Hannah and Aggie declined to sit, positioning themselves beside the game table and talking quietly while we waited for the others.

I stared at the rug beneath the game table, fighting a mild surge of panic. Roland's memories were shifting across my mind, louder since we'd descended the stairs into the room. They weren't taking over as usual, but they weren't shutting down. As casually as I could, I reached over and took Michael's hand. Unfortunately, nothing changed. I started to sort through excuses to leave.

I hadn't found a good one by the time Deidre, Chloe, and Melissa trooped down the narrow staircase into the room. That's the other thing. This room was completely sealed except for the staircase and two long, short windows high up on two of the walls.

As soon as we were all six in the same place, I felt it. Oh, I probably could have felt it before, but I guess I didn't want to. But in this place, with no other distractions, with an established circle of power right there, I felt the link of the coven quite clearly. It should have been comforting. I knew what a true coven was like. I'd been a member of one for a very short year right after high school. But this was different. This was flawed. In a true coven, power flowed freely between members. It often focused on the leader or the most powerful, but everyone possessed their fair share and everyone participated. But this was a farce. All of the focus was on me, and it was all one way. If I chose, I could pull energy from them and there wasn't a damn thing they could do about it. I remembered Roland's triumph at accomplishing this like it was my own. It made my skin crawl.

"Very well." Aggie stopped pacing at the edge of the Oriental rug, just above one of the inner rings of the circle of power. She faced me. "You discussed the legalities of the coven with Thomas yesterday, so you know that this house belongs to us, as a unit. If we dissolve the coven, all properties revert to various relatives of Roland's."

I smiled. "Damn relatives," I murmured.

If possible, Aggie's glare cooled. "They have been amply compensated. And they were not a part of Roland's daily life."

I nodded. "And your trouble is that he named me as part of the coven." That little piece had thrown me off guard. But then, Roland had been supremely confident that I'd be his, and he certainly hadn't expected to die.

"Indeed. Now, I'm sure we could work out an amicable settlement…"

"I don't want it."

That stopped her. "Excuse me?"

"I don't want it. Any of it. You can have Roland's money with my blessing."

Aggie blinked at me. She glanced at Chloe, who nodded. Then back at me. "You don't want your share?"

I shrugged, trying to smile while alien thoughts skittered in the forefront of my mind. "I don't have a share. You five had to live with him. You earned it." Ha! That caught them all off guard. But I meant it. "I don't want anything of Roland Parks's. I'm willing to do what's necessary to remove my name from the legal papers and to remove myself from the coven link."

"Just like that?" Hannah asked, a skeptical twist to her brows.

"Just like that."

Aggie's eyes narrowed. "How can we believe you?"

"I don't know. What can I do to convince you?"

"That's a *lot* of money," Melissa chimed in.

I glanced at her. True to form, Melissa had on worn jeans with patches of dirt at the knees that told me she'd been kneeling in the garden not too long before. Gardener's gloves were tucked into the waistband. Her short, reddish-blonde hair curled around her freckled face. "I know. I don't want it."

Aggie cleared her throat. "Correct me if I'm mistaken, but the coven is not so easily broken?"

I shrugged. "It won't be a cinch, no. This isn't a real coven, you realize. They're not normally central to just one person. What Roland did to you was a perversion."

Melissa and Hannah scowled. Chloe and Deidre lowered their gazes to their laps. Aggie showed no emotion whatsoever.

"Can you undo it?" Aggie asked.

"Yes."

"And you will?"

"Yes."

"But you'll wait until the legalities of the will are settled?"

I sighed. "Yes." I eyed her in the ensuing silence. "Don't thank me or anything."

"I don't know whether to trust you."

I shrugged, hopping down from the barstool. I had to get out of there and get rid of Roland's thoughts. "I don't know what I can do to make you believe me. I can only say that I don't want any of this. If I had my way, I'd never have met Roland Parks. I'd really like to go back to my life the way it was before." I took Michael's hand and turned a bright smile to Aggie. "We done?"

She frowned. "I don't understand you."

I shook my head, pulling Michael with me toward the staircase. "Don't try. Not many people do. You let me know when we can dissolve the coven, and I will."

Michael was quiet until we reached the top of the stairs. He put his arm around me as soon as we cleared them. "Memories?" he murmured.

I nodded, winding my arms around the solid bulk of his chest.

Hugging me to him, he steered us toward the kitchen.

"That was quick," Rudy said, grinning as he glanced over his shoulder. He stood at the sink, washing dishes.

"Yeah," Michael responded for us. "We need to go upstairs."

Rudy's grin faltered slightly, but he nodded. Quickly, he put the dish he was rinsing in the drainer, then moved to dry his hands.

The shifters at the table looked up, but said nothing as we departed through another door, the one that opened right on the main hall.

I was actually, I thought, okay. The memories weren't overpowering; they were just damn annoying. Telling me all sorts of things about the house and the people in it. Not anything important, like when Roland had met Shannon. It was this weird, constant babble in my head and this was a new kind of experience. I wasn't too worried. I just wanted it to stop.

Halfway up the sweeping staircase, a voice stopped us. "Hey, little witch."

Michael and I froze. Two steps below us, Rudy growled. We all turned to see Brent McMillian standing at the foot of the stairs.

Brent was a big, beefy man with the perfect build for a professional linebacker. His brown hair was like peach fuzz on the top of his square head, and perhaps a day's worth of stubble matched it on his equally square jaw. Brent had been Roland's leashed werewolf.

"Oh, what fresh new hell is this?" I muttered.

Brent mounted the first step, but Rudy's growl halted him. The two had fought twice, and Rudy had proven to be the stronger wolf both times, despite his smaller size. Of course, both fights had been interrupted by magical doings.

Brent only spared him a glance before focusing again on me. "I didn't want to believe it, but I felt it." He scowled. "You want to tell me why you've got my leash?"

Not until he mentioned it did I notice it. Amazed, I raised my right hand, skewed my sight to see magic, and gasped. Two thin yellow ropes of magic extended from my right palm toward Brent. Now that I saw them, I felt them. One of them circled his neck in a glow of yellow that only I saw, and the other would be snugged around the base of his dick.

Michael's hand on my shoulder tightened, and I glanced up at him. His eyes were fixed on my right hand. He could see it? Since when could he see magic?

I would have asked, but, gee, we had quite an audience for this. There was Shannon's shifter at the top of the stairs, the two shifters from the kitchen lounging in that doorway, listening, and, oh goodie, Aggie, Hannah, Deidre, and Chloe stepped out of the dining room to where they could be seen. It was a regular party.

So I answered Brent's question as best I could. "I...don't know." Brilliant, that's me.

"You *did* steal all of Roland's power!" Hannah screeched, pointing at me.

I glared at her.

"I'm not the only thing you kept?" Brent observed.

My glare switched to him. "I didn't keep you. I didn't even know about this—" I held out my hand, even though only Brent and I—oh, yeah, and Michael—could see it. "—until right now."

His hands fisted. "You mean you've held my leash for the last week and didn't even *know* it?"

Well, yeah, but it didn't seem prudent to stress that fact at the moment.

Hannah stepped farther into the room. "You stole all of his powers and his shapeshifter, and you expect us to believe that you'll just dissolve the coven?"

Well, wasn't she just a ton of fun? Now everyone knew about our private conversation. Wonder what the two enforcers would tell Howard Cook? Whoopee.

Aggie reached out to grab Hannah's arm and hush her, but the damage was done.

I decided I couldn't deal with them. After all, I had a *third* leash on my hands. How the hell was that even possible?

"Look here, little witch," Brent grumbled, clutching the banister in one beefy hand. "If you think that I'm going to be one of your boy toys, guess again." That got growls from Michael and Rudy. "I didn't even want to be Roland's shifter, and that sure as hell wasn't a sex thing."

"Oh, fuck you!" I spat, having had entirely enough of the whole lot of them. "Like I even *want* you."

The left side of his thin mouth raised in a snarl. "You've *got* me."

I heard a pained whine and glanced at Deidre, who stood in the corner of the hallway, wringing her hands. Deidre, who had a relationship with Brent. Who loved him, for all I knew.

Forget it. I didn't even think twice. I held out my hand, palm toward him, and dissolved the spell.

"Meg!" Michael hissed.

I ignored him, staring at a shocked Brent. "There. You're free." I turned my hand around and extended my middle finger. "Fuck off."

I turned, holding fast to Michael's hand, and headed back up the stairs. I left them all with those stupid pole-axed expressions and took my shifters to the safety of my room. My room. Ha! When had Roland's room become my room, and when the hell had it become a safe place?!

But it was. The only safe place in the house. We got into the room, and I thought up the sealing spell, both sound and lock this time. I wanted all of those people out of my life for at least a few hours.

I turned into Michael's chest and reached blindly back for Rudy. The blessed wolf came readily and folded himself around my back so that I was suffocating between two solid male bodies. I clutched the shirt lapels of the shifter in front of me and the hip of the one in back of me and shuddered. "It's too much," I whispered, sure that they heard me. "I can't take it."

Powerfully strong arms surrounded me. Rudy nuzzled my neck. Michael kissed the top of my head.

"Open up, Meg," Michael told me. "Let us help you."

Good idea. I let go of that internal lock that kept us pretty much separate. The thick ropes of magic that linked me to them flared to life, flooded with energy and emotions like rushing blood in veins. I was the heart, beating blood out of the arteries, but the conduits acted as veins as well, bringing the same back into me.

They got me to the bed, and we just lay there for a good long time, fully clothed. Yellow-orange magic surged around us, a blazing aura to those who could see it. For the moment, it was enough to simply be. To simply share.

"Can you see them?" I asked, cheek pressed to Michael's chest just beside his neck. "The memories?"

"Yes," Michael murmured.

"No," Rudy answered. He hugged me tighter. "But I would if I could, if it'd help you."

I squirmed around so that I faced him instead of Michael, taking that wickedly beautiful face in my hands. "Thank you." I kissed him softly.

"You're welcome." He kissed me back. "I love you."

I stared into those crystal-blue eyes and just barely managed not to parrot the words back. He was so earnest, but did I really love him? "Rudy, I..."

He smiled, kissing me softly again. "You don't have to say it, Meg. I know you love me. Just like I know Michael loves me." Kiss. "Just like I know he loves you." Kiss. "Neither of you is really comfortable saying it. Yet."

That right there was the magic of Rudy. How the hell could you manage *not* to love him? Especially when the conduits between us reinforced the emotions behind his words.

I closed my eyes and tucked my forehead underneath his chin, swallowing a knot of emotion.

He hugged me closer. I felt more than saw him stretch out his chin, encouraging and getting a soft kiss from Michael.

Roland subsided, burned out by the heat of awareness. Awareness of each other, of the bodies that were pressed so close together. Always before we'd needed sex to calm the memories, but never before had I so completely opened the leashes without sex. I couldn't read what they were thinking, but I felt what they were feeling. The mutual want between us was palpable.

I pressed my lips to the warm skin of Rudy's neck. Lapped out with my tongue to taste the salty spice of him.

The thick muscle of his neck worked, supporting his head as he deepened the kiss with Michael. Michael's hand slid up under the hem of my shirt to lightly caress my belly. Three pairs of legs entwined, straining to press three groins as close as possible.

"Clothes," I rasped.

As one, we broke from the embrace, each seeing to our own clothing. Rudy came back to me just as I was pulling my bra—my last piece of clothing—down my arms. Deftly, he caught it and twisted, trapping my wrists. At my wordless protest, he only grinned, using his makeshift handcuffs to lift my hands and pin them to the pillows above my head. He bore down with lips and body, keeping my protest to grunts and pinning the rest of me with his solid weight. I kissed him back, only mildly miffed at the denial of using my hands.

Rudy lifted a bit, and Michael's hand slid into the wetness between my legs. I know it was Michael's hand because Rudy's free hand plumped my breast, holding it for Michael to suckle. Hardly caring who was doing what, I spread my legs further, lifting one over Michael's bare hip to give him even better access.

They switched. Rudy bent to suckle my other breast and Michael took my mouth. Michael even took over holding down my hands. I protested a bit. Truthfully, I liked it. Take away all responsibility. Just let me feel. No doubt they got the gist of that through our connection.

Michael grumbled and pulled away, off the bed. I took the opportunity to free my hands, to Rudy's half-hearted protest.

Michael returned with a set of leather bondage cuffs. My eyes widened to see them. They were Roland's. A dozen disturbing memories skittered across my mind. None of them too disgusting physically. Roland hadn't been that much into true sadomasochism. He was more into dominance and submission, which, at the moment, to my embarrassment, I craved. How had Michael known where they were?

Michael held the cuffs up by the chain that connected them, waiting.

I swallowed and nodded.

Without a word, he strapped my wrists. Beside me, Rudy eyed the cuffs hungrily, and I recalled that this was something he had done before willingly. Professionally. He caught me watching and winked. "My turn next time," he whispered over my lips as Michael hung the short chain on a hook in the headboard.

My mind went curiously blank. It wasn't that they hadn't held me down before. They had. It wasn't that I was afraid of the cuffs. Truthfully, one thought of power and I could burst them. But I didn't want to. I felt weirdly alive with the cuffs on. Anticipation, perhaps.

Michael kissed my mouth, edging his knees between my thighs. He ran his hands down my sides, then trailed kisses down my front, pausing briefly to nuzzle and suck both my breasts.

Rudy bit my earlobe, assuring me in colorful terms that I looked hot and they were going to make me feel so good.

Michael spread my thighs with his hands and began a thorough, noisy feast on my wet, intimate flesh.

Whining happily, Rudy scurried down the bed. He actually pushed Michael over onto his side and eagerly wrapped first hands then mouth around Michael's cock. I watched helplessly, wrists twining in their bonds. The leashes, still wide open, gave us all an extra layer of pleasure.

I felt my orgasm ramping up, taunted and teased by Michael's assault on my swollen clit. My hips rocked uncontrollably and desperate mewls escaped my lips. I let the tension wash through the leashes, sharing, wanting them to know what they did to me as I lay bound to the bed.

Michael stopped us, pulling back from my clit with a pop. Desperate, I looked down to see one of his hands dig into Rudy's hair, yanking that eager mouth from his cock. Michael met my gaze. "I need to be inside you when I go."

I nodded eagerly.

He got up on his knees, grabbing my hips and dragging them up his thighs. He glanced at Rudy with a dark, wicked grin. "Get the lube and fuck me."

Rudy's eyes bugged out, matching, I'm sure, mine. We'd fucked many a time in many ways, but I'd yet to see Rudy take Michael. From the look of Rudy's surprise, it didn't seem to be a common occurrence.

Not that he wasn't game, of course. Rudy rolled from the bed.

I couldn't track his movements very well, however, because Michael turned his attention back to spearing me on his monster cock. I groaned as he worked it inside me. Even wet as I was, it took some doing. He adjusted us so that my butt was flush on the bed, his huge, beautiful body poised above me as he slowly pulled out and shoved back in. Out and in. Out and in. Goddess, that felt amazing!

He stopped. I managed to screw open my eyes to see Rudy behind him. I couldn't see exactly what he was doing, but I could guess well enough. I watched Michael's face. Saw the first twinge of pain that made his cock twitch inside me. Saw the pain quickly dissolve and felt the echo of a pure rush of black, inky pleasure that rushed up his spine as Rudy slid slowly in.

"Goddess, Mike," Rudy whispered, one hand clutching Michael's shoulder, the other his waist.

Michael pulled back from me, pushing himself onto Rudy. From the twin groans that burbled from my and Rudy's throats, you'd think Michael was doing all the fucking. But then, he was. He always was. No matter what we did, Michael led. That was just a rule of our little trio. Michael lowered himself further atop me, down now on his elbows, and opened cat eyes on me. His dark smile showed pointed teeth. The hands that slid beneath my back to grip my shoulders from beneath had talons.

I gasped, overwhelmed by the raw animal lust that poured through the leashes. Above Michael, Rudy yipped, and I looked up and saw the hand on Michael's shoulder was slightly furred and tipped with black claws. If I'd had a beast, I think I'd have slipped into the change as well. As it was, my skin felt wrong on my body. As though it were the wrong size.

"It goes both ways, Meg," Michael growled, lisping slightly through overlong teeth. His hips worked gorgeous cock into me, punching a hole in my heart. "Give and take." He lowered his head to snuffle my neck. "Will you take?"

"Goddess, yes!" I cried, not even thinking about my answer.

The leashes were alive, ropes of power that looped around us, shining tightly, pulsing wetly with crimson arousal.

I writhed underneath them, just at the brink of explosion. Panting, sheened with sweat, I hurled my hips at him, aching to burst. But it didn't come. I needed... *we* needed...

A copper taste filled my mouth. Eagerly, I latched onto Michael's mouth and the lip he'd bitten. *Blood!* Yes! That's what we needed. I let the fluid pour down my throat, knowing it was only a piece, it was only part. We also needed...

Pleasure detonated when Rudy's teeth dug into the flesh of Michael's shoulder and blood hit his throat. Our screams were muted, mine and Michael's echoing in our fused mouths and Rudy's shattering against Michael's shoulder. The leashes expanded like a mushroom cloud, far too bright and too complex for me to work out, and my mind was far too drenched in brutal ecstasy for me to try. It went on for ages, tearing us apart and remaking us from inside. Fear and love and wonderment all coalesced into a whole that couldn't immediately be recognized as three separate beings.

I collapsed back, desperately trying to remember how to breathe. Michael was braced on hands and knees over me, lungs laboring as sweat and blood dripped onto my chest. I could just make out Rudy from where he sprawled across Michael's back, breathing audible through his open mouth.

"One of…" I tried. Lost my ability to speak. Swallowed and tried again. "One of these days…we're just going to have…nice, normal sex, right?" Swallowed again. "Without it nearly killing us?"

Michael groaned, pushing up slightly.

Rudy echoed the groan and slid off Michael's back to a heap beside us. Light brown hair hid his eyes, but his sated smile was clearly evident.

"Maybe," Michael breathed, pushing back farther until he sat on his heels. He raised a hand to his mouth, swiping a thumb across the blood that dribbled out of the corner.

The position and the fact that his cock hadn't softened fully meant he was still inside me. My inner walls twitched, and I groaned at the spasm of delight that ripped up my spine.

I stopped. Froze. "What the hell?" Something was different.

Carefully, I took stock. I licked my lips, tasted blood. Michael's blood. Okay, yeah, that was new. The three or four times blood had been part of our lovemaking, they'd taken bites out of me. But I'd only asked it to feed the leash spell. This time I hadn't done anything to feed the spell, just let it flare. I blinked. What the…?

I stared up at Michael. He lapped slowly at the cut he'd put in his own lower lip, watching me intently. His eyes shifted to Rudy for a moment, then back to me.

My skin still tingled, and now I was afraid it was more than just afterglow. "What did you do?"

"I'm not sure yet," he confessed.

My eyes went wide. "What?"

I tried to sit up, hampered by the bonds that still held my hands over my head. I did manage to shimmy off of Michael's thighs and up into a pseudo-seated position with my wrists about at my chin and my elbows bent just before me. I twisted my sight just that much to allow me to see magic better and gasped again.

Four new, sunny ropes extended from Michael's body—two from his heart and two from the base of his groin. The thick, strong ropes extended toward Rudy and me—Rudy's cock and neck, my groin and neck.

"You *leashed* us?!"

Rudy pushed up on his elbow, his other hand splayed over his chest. "Is that what I felt?"

I gaped at Michael. "You *leashed* us?!"

He grew a profoundly pleased smile on his swollen lips. "It would seem so."

"But you can't..."

He raised a sweaty brow at me. "I did."

"But...but *how?* You're not a witch."

He sat back, wincing slightly as he settled on his butt. "I drew on your power."

"What?"

"It's happened gradually since you first leashed me. Being in this house made it more intense. I was able to sense your power and Roland's much more keenly here." He smiled at me. "I think I've managed to subdue most of Roland's memories for you until this afternoon."

"And you didn't mention that until now?"

He grimaced at me. "You're welcome."

"Michael!"

He shrugged. "I wasn't sure it was really happening until yesterday, and there hasn't been a chance to tell you since then."

I blinked. So that was why the memories hadn't taken me over. But…"You can work spells?"

"It looks like it."

I just managed not to say that was impossible. The man made an absolute art of proving the impossible to be quite possible. "But you can't leash a witch."

"You leashed me."

"You're a shifter."

"Born a witch."

"*I'm* not a shifter."

"And yet I managed to leash you."

I swallowed. "It doesn't *work* that way."

"I'll admit, I didn't think it would work with you. I think the fact that you were completely open helped. Your leashes led the way, so to speak. I copied what you'd done." He winced again as he rolled off the bed. He was being entirely too casual about something so profound!

I glanced at Rudy, who simply lay on his back, eyes shut, fingers lightly playing in the sweat that was cooling on his flat belly. If he were a cat, he'd be purring.

Why was I the only one disturbed by this? "You can't leash a shifter twice," I called after Michael as he disappeared into the bathroom.

He reappeared in seconds with two dry towels. "I think I managed that because of the link we already had through you." He threw one towel on top of Rudy and used the other to dry himself.

Rudy grinned up at him.

Michael smiled and winked.

I watched them in horror. "Why?" I finally asked the important question.

Michael knelt on the bed beside my bent legs, but didn't try to touch me yet. Instead he smoothed a hand over Rudy's calf, almost petting him. "Were you going to hand me over to Shannon?"

"What?"

"That's what Shannon wanted to talk to you about, isn't it? Me?"

I blinked. So much had happened today that I just realized that I hadn't gotten to tell them about my talk with Shannon. "Yes."

"What did she offer you?"

I pulled at the cuffs that bound my wrists. "Take these off."

"In a minute."

"Take them off."

He glowered. "Break them open yourself if you're that pissed. Otherwise, answer my question."

My jaw dropped.

"What did she offer you?"

"She offered to speak for me at the tribunal."

"If you gave me to her."

"Yes."

"Did you consider it?"

"You said yourself she couldn't hold you."

"Did you consider it?"

"I'd be lying if I said I didn't."

"Ha!"

"I told her no, damn it!"

"On top of that, just today I watched you blithely give up a coven focused on you, an inheritance worth millions, and a third leashed shifter, all without blinking an eye."

Gee, say it like that…"I don't want all that."

"Which means you deserve every bit of it."

"What?"

He shook his head, reaching for my wrists. The cuffs were straps and buckles, not locks. "None of this is going away, Meg, no matter how much you wish it. Even if you give away everything you could get from Roland, even if you reject that you could hold at least one more shifter, even if you never step foot out of your house again, things like this are going to find you."

My hands fell free one by one, and I rubbed them, staring at him mutinously. Wisely, he sat back and left the towel at my side.

"You're a dangerously powerful instinctive, Meg. You said so yourself right after we first met, when we were trying to figure out what to do to get your magic back from Roland. Magic isn't your craft. It isn't something you choose to do. It's something you *have* to do. You have to make it not happen."

"That doesn't explain why you leashed me."

"I leashed you to take away one of your options. So you couldn't get rid of us."

Rudy pushed up onto his elbows, intently listening to the exchange.

"I wasn't," I protested weakly, unable to meet Michael's gaze.

"But you were tempted. Don't say that you weren't."

I snatched up the towel and used it to swipe at the sweat that had mostly dried on my chest. I wasn't sure if the cinch around my neck and clit were really tingling, or if I just imagined they were because I was hyper-aware that they were there. Or maybe Michael was tugging on them, testing them. I wasn't going to ask him.

Michael sighed and stretched out across the width of the bed, pillowing his head on Rudy's thigh. "I leashed you as part of what I need to do to protect you. To force you to use the powers you can't deny."

Rudy balanced on one elbow and reached down to comb his fingers through the sweaty tendrils of Michael's hair.

I scowled. "That's fucking convoluted logic."

Michael shrugged. "But it's true. I also leashed you to give you another way to share that power with us. It seems to help you."

I finished with the towel and hugged the terry softness to my chest, glowering at him. "Why do you care? You could have let me release you and never seen me again."

"And lose the only access to magic I've had or am probably ever going to get?"

"Mike!" Rudy snapped, smacking the top of his head.

The bottom dropped out of my world. I tried to hold on to my anger, but despair bloomed up behind it, cooling it. "Is that all I am to you?"

Rudy sat up, forcing Michael to sit, too. "No, Meg, don't listen to him. He—"

"That's not all." Michael said, talking over Rudy. "But that's all you're likely to believe." He leaned forward, on hands and knees before me, gaze locked with mine. "I'm not like Rudy. I can't believe in falling in love so quickly. Any more than you can. I do like you, very much, and I do care about you. I don't want to see you hurt. I *do* want to see you through this and out of it. But I'm a realist. You and I both get something out of this relationship. You get someone willing to watch out for you and help you curb your instinctive magic. I get to personally work magic for the first time in my life. These are benefits both you and I can accept." He put on a wicked grin. "Outside of fabulous sex."

I tried to get angry, but I couldn't. His words made sense. I hadn't been able to say words of love any easier than he had. Like he said, the reasons he gave worked for both of us. "Okay. I can buy all that."

"Gee, how romantic," Rudy grumbled. He rolled over and off the bed. "I'm going to take a shower."

Michael reached out to brush my jaw gently with his fingertips, but he seemed to be out of words. He rolled off the other side of the bed and disappeared into the surveillance closet.

Chapter Eleven

The rest of that night was the strangest we had spent together so far. Rudy took a shower, then joined me on the big bed to watch television. After a while, I got up and took a shower, then rejoined him to watch a movie. Michael took his own shower not long afterward and joined us. We were all mostly quiet, like we'd made a deal to not talk about anything. At some point, Rudy decided we were hungry and went down to the kitchen. He was gone long enough that the movie we'd been watching ended.

Finally I'd had enough. I kept my eyes on the scrolling credits and asked, "So, what are we going to do?"

"I don't think there's much we can do." Michael sat beside me, both of us propped up on the pillows against the massive headboard. We didn't touch, but I felt his solid warmth.

"Do you think your leashing trick will help?"

"I do. If it doesn't spread Roland's power more evenly between us, it should at least be odd enough to camouflage the abundance. After all, to our knowledge no one's ever leashed a witch before. Even the grand leaders should be confused on how much power that would create."

"Especially if one of the witches is also a shifter." I sighed, wiping a hand over my face. "I'm having a hard enough time with what's happening to me. I can't *imagine* what this is like for you."

He lifted his arm and draped it across my shoulders, drawing me against his side and the warm, fragrant luxury of his skin. "I've lived with being a shifter and witch most of my life." He kissed the top of my head. "Thanks to you, I actually get to *be* a witch for the first time. No matter what, that's precious to me."

I got that warm, fuzzy feeling and knew I wore a goofy grin. I snuggled up under his arm to hide it.

I had to get up to let Rudy in with our dinner cart. The three of us discussed the tribunal and what we'd do and say while we ate. Despite the topic of conversation, it was actually a pleasant meal.

I cracked a yawn as we crawled into bed after finishing dinner. "Can we just watch another movie or something tonight? I'm not sure I'm up for having sex again."

Rudy sighed. "Lightweight."

I threw a pillow at him, which made him laugh.

Michael chuckled. "I think we can do that. As long as we don't make a habit of it."

I threw another pillow at him.

So, okay, the day after tomorrow a few of the most powerful witches in the world were gathering to see if I needed to be put to death for a crime I happened to have committed, but tonight I was happy.

Go figure.

Chapter Twelve

I have no idea what time it was when it started. Sometime in the deep of night, since we were all three asleep. I didn't know what was happening. I woke up, feeling nauseous. I flopped back from my spot draped over Rudy's back, shoulder to shoulder with Michael, who lay on his back. The hand he'd had resting on my hip ended up on my thigh and he squeezed it softly. I stared up at the darkness above my face, trying to figure out why I felt…

I popped up to sit, hand going over my mouth when I thought I was going to heave. It turned out to be dry, but the sudden movement made me dizzy.

Michael sat up.

Rudy rolled over. "What's wrong?"

I shook my head, hand still over my mouth, the other arm wrapped around my middle. This wasn't normal. This wasn't just nausea. "Something's wrong."

Michael grabbed my shoulders and made me face him.

I groaned, eyes squinching shut as my stomach rolled again. I tried to turn my face up to his, but my head seemed way too heavy for my neck. It fell back.

Rudy turned on the light.

Michael spread his hand over the back of my skull, supporting as he lifted it slowly. "You're weak."

"Yeah."

"Magic?"

I hadn't thought of that yet. "Dunno, I…Goddess, I'm gonna…pass out."

Michael's leashes on me flared to life. Through them, he poured energy into me. Enough so that I could hold up my own head. Enough so that I could think straight to take stock of myself. Not enough to make the feeling go away. "I feel like I'm being drained."

"Maybe you are." Michael took hold of my head with both hands and held me steady, our eyes locked together. "Show me."

I didn't so much show him as let go. He was already intimately connected with me, metaphysically speaking. All he had to do was start to look.

I managed to follow.

We both saw it at about the same time.

"Damn," he swore, pushing away from to me to climb out of bed. He sped for the surveillance closet.

"Those bitches," I snarled, falling over Rudy in my haste to get out of bed, too. My limbs felt like they were made of jelly.

"Someone want to fill me in?" Rudy asked, helping me gain my feet, then steadying me when I got there.

"The coven," I explained as he helped me grab up my clothes and get dressed. "They're down in the game room. They must have invoked the circle of power that's tuned to me. They're draining me."

"Draining you?"

"Magic."

"Is that why your leash feels weird?"

I skewed my sight that bit and looked at him. The leashes that bound him to me were dim, almost sputtering. "Yeah."

"What do they think they're doing?"

"Not sure." I stumbled back onto the bed. He knelt before me with my shoes, but I waved him away. "No, get dressed."

"We're going down there?"

"We've got to."

Michael stormed from the surveillance closet, headed for his own clothes. "They're down there, all right. The cameras don't pick up the magic, but they're in the circle and they're chanting." He paused, glancing at me as he pulled on a T-shirt. "I almost recognize the spell."

"What?"

"From Roland's memories."

I had to struggle to think. The energy from Michael was helping, but I was still being drained. "Are they doing to me what he did to them?"

"That's the idea."

"Damn!"

"One more piece of bad news," he said, stepping into his jeans.

"Shit. What?"

"Shannon's with them."

"Shannon?! What's she doing here?"

"Let's go find out."

We trooped out the door with Michael in the lead, Rudy hanging back to help me. I was walking on my own, but I was kind of shaky.

The shifter at the end of the hall wasn't the foxy one from earlier that day. He was much bigger. He stood from his chair as we charged toward the stairs. "Stop right there."

"No," Michael growled. I was behind him, so I couldn't see if he had eyes and claws to go with that growl.

Evidently he did and the shifter took offense. The guy brought up beefy arms with hands that had turned to thick, round paws. "I said stop." His face half changed as he spoke, gaining the eyes and teeth of a bear.

"I said no!" Michael didn't attack him physically. He used one of my tricks and threw a blast of raw power at the man. It was the spell of a lazy or untrained witch, brute force with little finesse, but with enough juice to it, it was quite effective.

Now, shifters are somewhat immune to magical attacks, especially ones like that. But the guy wasn't expecting it from Michael. Me, maybe, but not another shifter. He tumbled back over his chair, stunned.

Michael's hurried walk didn't even falter. He glanced over his shoulder to make sure we were still following, and then I saw the cat eyes and fangs. Is it bad that despite our situation, that kind of excited me? Probably.

I was able to race down the stairs, but Rudy held me up. I was smart enough to let him.

Michael reached the bottom of the staircase just as two more shifters blocked his path. Shannon's shifters. These weren't the enforcers sent by Howard Cook. Damn!

Michael delayed them with another blast of power, but these guys didn't go down like the first. In that flash of non-light, first Michael, then one of the shifters, changed forms. Michael's clothes fell empty to the staircase, and his jaguar body wrapped around a spotted leopard—at least, I'm pretty sure it was a leopard. Maybe it was another jaguar. Regardless, he was another cat, and they tore into each other with angry, feline shrieks.

Rudy let go of my arm and hurled himself down the last few stairs, changing in mid-flight to land in a heap with the other shifter. The guy tumbled him, turning into another spotted cat.

I stumbled to a stop, just barely avoiding the jeans that had fallen from Rudy's changing body. I grabbed onto the banister, catching my breath. Two snarling, dangerous fights blocked my path to where I needed to go. Worse, I had this gnawing need to help Michael, thanks to his leash, but I didn't have a clue what I could do. A glance over my shoulder showed me that the bear guy had recovered and was on his way down. Shit.

Boldly trusting my legs, I darted sideways into the kitchen. I stumbled once to my knees, but managed to make it through one door, then into the dining room just as the bear made the kitchen. I paused in the dining room, just inside the arch that let me see the other side of the two snarling shifter battles. Rudy and one cat were circling, growling. Michael's back was to me, one black paw lifted to swipe at the cat who crouched before him.

Quickly, I pulled energy, knowing it came through Michael and sorry for it, but I needed it. As the bear came through the door from the kitchen, I hurled a spell at him, barking a word of power. It wasn't a spell I'd ever learned, but it was one that Roland could do without thought. A magical net, barely seen but definitely felt, closed around him and squeezed. He fell with a thud. Giving him no more thought, I turned and barked twice more, aiming at Shannon's shifters. I caught the one stalking Rudy, but the one before Michael saw what I did, turned, and ran.

My bleeding shifters turned toward me, speeding on four furry legs each to me. Rudy hovered beside me, leaning his strong shoulder against my hip as I started to sag. Michael brushed past me to the door to the game room on the lower level.

As I was the only one with opposable thumbs at the moment, I opened the door. Michael shot through, pouring into the shadows of the narrow staircase. I started to follow, but my legs gave out on me. Crying out faintly, I grabbed at the doorframe. Strong, strange hands caught my wrist and lifted me into the air. I blinked up into the face of a wolf mounted atop a hugely muscled neck and shoulders. In the shadowed light, I couldn't quite make out a color, but I'm pretty sure all that fur was a light, tawny brown. Arms cradled me against the shorter fur that covered the werewolf's chest. I'd never seen either of my shifters in were form—half human, half beast—but I knew this was Rudy. It had to be Rudy. It kind of *looked* like Rudy, in a really odd sense. If it wasn't, I wouldn't feel perfectly safe in his embrace. If it wasn't, I wouldn't feel the faint trace of my fading leash on him. He cradled me gently, then fairly flew down the dark steps to the game room floor.

Proximity to the spell that drained me didn't help or hurt me. The game table and all its chairs had been shoved against the wall, the rug rolled up. Six women stood in a pulsing blue circle of power. The candle sconces along the walls were lit—electricity had strange effects on spells and was best not used around magic—but their light was paltry in comparison to the spell. They chanted words that I recognized through Roland. Indeed it was the spell that he'd used to weaken a witch just before he made her his.

Well, wait. That's not quite right. Three of them chanted. Three of them were on their hands and knees, heads sagging forward between their shoulders. I recalled a memory of Roland's, seeing this circle in a similar state. Chloe, Melissa, and Deidre were being drained to give the circle power. This was *normal* for this so-called coven. Almost. None of Roland's memories showed me Aggie or Hannah participating in the spell. Bitches were doing unto others what Roland had done unto them. Hadn't they heard of the golden rule?

Michael's sleek, four-footed body paced on the near side of the circle, his darkness silhouetted against the neon-blue glow emanating from the circle. The circle and the runes etched in it all rose like steady flames about a foot and a half off the ground.

Rudy set me down beside one of the big chairs that matched the sofa, waiting a brief moment to see if I could stand on my own. When he saw that I could, he stepped back to the single doorway, glancing up the stairs. He shut the door, then stayed by it, guarding.

At the other side of the circle, just behind Deidre, Brent crouched in werewolf form. He snarled toward us, gleaming, pointed teeth evident in the blue glow, then dropped fearfully angry eyes back down at Deidre's slumped back.

I stepped toward the circle, a hand out toward it. Blue light shimmered before me, and the part nearest me bulged outward. I tried to connect to it, to take control, but although the circle was tuned to me, a strong enough witch had bound it from me.

I had to do something, but I wasn't sure what. "Shannon, what do you think you're doing?"

She lowered her chin and met my gaze. To her credit, her chant didn't waver, but her eyes were big. Well, I couldn't blame her. Her spell should've had me comatose in the bed upstairs. It would have if I hadn't had Michael and Roland's power to draw from. I imagine she was a tad confused about why I was up and walking.

Hannah, whose back was to us, turned, saw Michael, and screamed. The spell faltered, and I felt a sluggish spill of power back into me.

Aggie grabbed her arm, glaring as she chanted.

Hannah, eyes wide, swallowed quickly, then picked up the chant.

The trickle of energy back into me wasn't nearly enough for me to gain from it. I sank to my knees on the hard brick floor, not wanting to expend the energy to try to stay upright.

Michael padded back to my side, nudging that great, black head against my shoulder.

I wrapped my arms around his neck, digging fingers into the inky fur. "I can't," I whispered.

In a flash, he changed to his were form. He crouched down on hugely muscled limbs to keep his position in my circled arms.

I pulled back and he met my gaze, eyes fully feline and face mostly so as well. But the voice was familiar, even if it lisped. "You said the circle was keyed to you. Can you break it?"

I had to blink twice at him, then looked around his shoulder at the glowing blue. I felt the connection clear as day, but control had been wrenched from me by a stronger hand. "Not enough juice."

"Even from me?"

"It would drain you."

"So drain me."

I looked at those cat eyes, so intent. "I can't harm you like that."

"It'll harm me more if they drain you to death!" He shook me, clawed hands digging into my shoulders. "Do it!"

I gulped. "The leash. I can't...put you in danger."

"What?"

"Leash, damn it. I'm compelled to *protect* you!"

He growled and spun around, gathering me into his lap as he crouched on the floor. It was frightening how strong he was. He held my full weight in the crook of one arm without hardly thinking about it. In human form, he was pretty darn strong, but in this form...Goddess!

I dug my fingers into his fur, eyes closed. What could I do? What could we do? Recklessly, I dove into Roland's memories, searching out those of how and when he'd made this circle. How he'd formed his warped coven. "Wait. There's something I can try."

"What?"

I tried to push from his arms to my feet, but was too weak to accomplish it.

He gave me an impatient look and gathered me back. "What are you doing?"

"Take me over there. By Chloe."

Michael carried me and set me on my knees behind Chloe. At a little direction from me, he scooted me over until I was enough to her right that I could see her face through the blue haze.

I glanced up. Shannon glared daggers at me, but her chin was still lifted and her chant didn't falter. If anything, she picked up speed.

I swallowed. "Chloe." My voice was starting to get raspy.

She didn't move.

I opened my mouth to call again, but Michael beat me to it. "Chloe!"

Chloe's jumped slightly. Her head rolled, and I saw those big doe eyes peering at me from beneath the hang of her hair.

I reached out a hand, palm up, fingers spread. The circle was something like heat to my palm. It didn't burn, but I didn't dare touch it. It was a heated awareness that wanted to reach me. Wanted, but was held back by Shannon's steely control. "Help me. Take my hand."

"What are you doing?" Michael demanded.

I ignored him, not having enough time or energy to explain. I shook my hand at the other woman. "Please, Chloe. Help me, and you'll never have to go through this again."

It was the only way. If I could get her to take my hand, I could use the fact that the circle and the coven were still tuned to me and maybe turn the tide of power in my direction. Or just break the spell. But unless I could get her to break the circle, it was hopeless.

She stared at me through the lank tendrils of her hair, her eyes as big and innocent as a cartoon bunny. "Please, Chloe."

Slowly, she lifted one hand from the stone beside her knee and raised it to me, fingers extended.

"No!" Shannon screamed, immediately picking up the chant after the utterance. My advantage was that she had to remain where she was to keep up the draining spell.

Chloe cringed, glancing at her.

"No, Chloe!" Michael barked. "Take Meg's hand."

His authoritative voice did it. Chloe was nothing if not obedient. She turned away from Shannon, leaning toward me.

The chant broke. Shannon stalked across the circle, snatching up Chloe's hand. The blue of the circle fell, the light now limited to the designs on the floor rather than the tall, steady flame. Aggie and Hannah's voices faltered, unsure how to proceed with Shannon out of place. The circle held, holding Michael and me out, but the spell inside it had broken.

The drain on me halted, but nothing trickled back. Determined, I raised my head to glare at Shannon.

Her nostrils flared. "You will *not* have this. I won't allow it."

I refused to let despair show in my face. As long as she was in the circle, we couldn't get to her, but she couldn't start up another spell without leaving Chloe in place. The hand I extended started to fall.

Another hand shot out to clutch mine. I twisted my head that little bit to see that Melissa had managed to turn around and crawl over while Shannon was distracted by grabbing Chloe. Defiant, Melissa met my gaze and gripped my fingers.

Then we screamed.

Caught off guard, I didn't have the power poised to take back the circle. Shannon's protective seal remained, not scalding our flesh, but searing our auras in hot cobalt where we crossed it. Only shock kept our fingers entwined. I couldn't think clearly, so I certainly couldn't direct the necessary energy at breaking the circle.

Michael surged to the rescue. He seized the power and shoved it through me. Like a tidal wave, it rushed down my arm and smashed into the circle. It widened the gap made by my and Melissa's hands.

"Meg," he gritted, voice pained.

Right. The circle was keyed to me. As much as he was linked to me, I was the one who needed to direct it. I took control from him and concentrated on the circle. A green pulse flashed across the runes as the earth magic flared to life. I had to fight Shannon's midnight control, but with the circle now turned back where it belonged, she lost her hold. She'd fallen back a few steps to the far edge of the circle. She tried valiantly to hold. She tried to turn the circle against me, but I'd already taken back control.

Blue power winked out in a flash of forest green before the light went out entirely.

Melissa slumped forward, falling against Michael's thigh, unconscious, with her fingers still threaded in mine.

I slumped with her, bending over her back as Michael's surge of strength drained from me.

"Damn you!" Shannon screamed, the hysterical note in her voice entirely unlike her. She sounded mad, both of the angry and the insane varieties. "This won't happen!"

I felt her gathering a spell, like electricity on my skin. I tried to turn my head to see her. To see it. Tried to dredge up some modicum of power for a shield, but there was nothing more to pull. I had nothing. She was going to have me.

Michael scrambled over us, putting his huge black body between me and Shannon. I gasped, falling across Melissa's back. I screamed with Michael when he took the brunt of Shannon's raw bolt of shearing white power. It seeped into his skin like molten lava, and only his being a shifter kept it from torching him.

"You can't have it all!" she screeched, throwing another bolt. "Not this time!"

Michael managed to put up a shield between him and Shannon, a blessed disc of hazy gray. Since he was bigger than either me or Melissa, it was plenty large enough to shield us all and deflect the white-hot energy around us to sink into the wall behind. The bolts were keyed to living matter, meaning the furniture and room would be none the worse for wear even if Shannon managed to set us aflame.

"You can't always be stronger. You can't always be right. Not this time!" Another bolt cracked toward us, shattering to a billion rays across Michael's shield. "I don't know how you escaped Roland, but you won't escape me. This time I'll be rid of you once and for all."

Michael's shield cracked. It wasn't a very strong shield, nor particularly well made. It showed inexperience in such things.

I took a breath, trying to force my body up so I could help him with the shield.

"Why does everyone flock to you? Why does everyone *protect* you?!"

Bam! Another hit. This one made Michael cry out. I felt the echo of scorching pain, and it was enough to make me cry. We weren't going to be able to take much more of this.

I reached for Michael's furry back, determined, at least, to lend what energy I could. Not at all sure where I'd find it.

"Why—?" Shannon screamed, abruptly cut off to a gurgling end. I'm pretty sure I heard flesh tear.

Confused, I fell to the side, needing to see around Michael's huge body.

Shannon's bleeding corpse gaped at me from within Rudy's tawny werewolf arms. He released razor-sharp talons from her neck and loosened his grip, letting her drop to the floor. The blood dripping from his claws was black in the dim candlelight.

"Rudy," I breathed. "No."

Hannah screamed that hysterical shriek of a woman beyond reason.

Rudy hadn't heard me. He leapt over Shannon's body, bounding on powerful arms and legs to catch Aggie, who had just made it to the stairs. The woman only got a chance to cry out once before he slashed at her back.

"Goddess!" I cried.

From the corner of my eye, I saw Brent, still in werewolf form, dart up behind Hannah, claws out. I turned my head, reeling, still suffering from the energy drain.

Black arms snatched me up, turning me into a chest of equally black fur. I tried to push away, but Michael held me, not allowing me to see any more of what was happening.

Hannah's scream cut off, accompanied by a sickening snap of bone.

More screaming. Who? Oh, it was me. Screaming into the solid wall of Michael's chest.

Tears streaming down my face, body feeling light and somehow disconnected, I slumped in his arms. "No. Oh, no."

The world blanked out.

Chapter Thirteen

I woke to find a stranger bending over me. He was classic Native American in looks, complete with long black hair in two thick braids. The hair was shot through with gray, but his face could have been of a man in his twenties. He wore a faded green plaid shirt and jeans.

I started and he smiled. "You're back," he said, patting my hand where it rested on my belly.

I recognized the inside of the canopy of Roland's bed, along with the gold and brown cover. Lemon silk sheets were tucked up under my armpits. I had on an extra large T-shirt—one of Michael's, I think—but I'm pretty sure I was naked otherwise.

"Who are you?"

The bed moved beside me, and I realized why I wasn't too panicked. Turning my head, I saw Rudy stretched out on top of the covers beside me, head pillowed on his arm. Typical of Rudy, he wore jeans and nothing else. There was a nasty, healing gash on the upper left part of his chest. Unlike in stories, shifters don't heal instantly when they shift, although they do tend to heal faster and can take more damage than a normal human. A myriad of fading scratches marked his arms and shoulders, with one set of thin lines across his left cheek. He smiled, reaching out to stroke the line of my jaw with two fingers. "Hey."

"Hey."

"You feel okay?"

I glanced at the man seated to my left, then back at Rudy. He didn't seem worried, so I decided the guy, at least, was all right. "Shouldn't I feel okay?"

"You've been out for a day and a half."

"What?"

He nodded, edging closer so he could comfortably rest his hand on mine on my belly. "T.C. says you should be all right, though. He says you just need to restore your energy."

"T.C.?"

Rudy gestured with his chin at the guy. "This is T.C. He's the Mexican grand dame's spirit healer."

Day and a half. My eyes went wide. "The tribunal!"

"It's going on right now."

"What?!" I tried to sit up, but the bed—no, the *room*— spun.

Two sets of male hands easily pushed me back down.

"Easy there," said T.C. as he straightened the sheets around me. Wow, he had a nice voice. Deep and resonant— kind of like Michael's. "You're not ready to get up yet."

"But the tribunal."

T.C. nodded, then stood. Whoa, he was tall, too. "I'll go tell them you're awake. They'll want to talk to you." He stared at me for another moment, an odd smile on his face.

Long enough for me to frown. "What?"

"You're quite a witch."

"I am?"

He laughed, as though we shared a joke, then turned and left.

I watched him leave, baffled by what he'd said.

"You hungry?" Rudy asked, pushing to his elbow.

I turned and looked up at him. Last I'd seen him, he'd been in werewolf form and he'd killed two women.

He frowned. "What is it? What's wrong, Meg?"

I closed my eyes and swallowed. "N-nothing. Just...what's happened?"

He rubbed his hand on my shoulder, and I tried really hard to not remember that same hand ripping open Aggie's back. "You passed out and Michael brought you up here. Shannon's shifters gave us some grief, but then those enforcers showed up and helped get everything under control. Shannon had spelled them in their rooms. Melissa says she was going to blame that on you. She was going to blame a lot of shit on you, Meg." He lifted my hand to his lips, kissed it, then continued. "The grand leaders showed up this morning."

"What time is it?"

"Four."

I opened my eyes. Sunlight pushed through the drawn sheers of the window, so he couldn't mean four a.m. "They've been here all day?"

Rudy nodded.

"What have they been saying? Who have they been talking to?"

"I don't know. I had to testify once, but Michael was up here with you during that. Other than that, I've been here with you. T.C.'s a good enough guy, but I couldn't leave you alone."

"Where's Michael?"

"Downstairs."

"Alone?"

He sighed. "I can only protect one of you at a time, Meg. Of the two, he was a bit more capable of looking out for himself."

I sighed. "I know. I didn't mean…" I shook my head, raising a hand to cover my eyes. "You testified?"

"Well, I did kill a grand dame."

That made me look at him, my heart stuttering.

His eyes were trained on me, all levity leeched from their crystal-blue depths. "She was going to kill you, Meg. I had to kill her."

I pulled in a trembling breath. "No. Shannon's not like that…She…"

I trailed off as he shook his head. "I don't know what world you're trying to live in, Meg, but she had it in for you.

She was going to kill you, and she was going to kill Michael at the very end. She had to die."

I swallowed. "Aggie—"

"Was going to do the same."

"No. She wasn't strong enough."

"Meg, she would have killed you that first day if she could have. That woman was a danger to you. She had to die."

I stared at that strangely innocent face, at his boyish good looks. Despite his solemn tone and serious words, I just couldn't see a murderer there. "What did the tribunal say?"

He shrugged. "Don't know. They haven't said anything yet. They've just been questioning everyone."

The door opened and Michael came in. Dressed in casual slacks and a vibrant emerald shirt that did wonders for his eyes, he looked good enough to eat. Even with a two healing slashes across his temple. When he sat on the bed and took my face in his hands to pull me into a kiss, I did my best to eat him.

"How do you feel?" he asked when he pulled away.

"Tired. Confused."

He smiled that beautiful smile that always managed to stutter my heart. "I would imagine. Are you up for seeing the tribunal?"

"I don't know. You've been with them; you tell me. Am I?"

He nodded, dislodging a lock of hair from behind his left ear. "I think you are. I think you'll be pleased." He drew back. "Mostly."

"Mostly?"

He shook his head. "No time to explain. They're waiting."

I started to push myself up, but he pushed me back down.

"Wait. Rudy, can you get her some better clothes?"

I looked down at the T-shirt I wore. The covers had fallen back enough for me to confirm that I was indeed naked other than the shirt.

While Rudy did so, I grabbed Michael's arm. "Michael, tell me what's been happening."

He patted my hand. "Mostly questions around Shannon's death."

I dug into his muscle with my fingernails.

He smiled and patted my hand again. "Don't worry. We've all been absolved."

"We have?"

"Self-defense. Melissa, Chloe, Deidre, and Brent all testified that Shannon, Aggie, and Hannah planned to drain every ounce of your power in an effort to trap me."

"They did?"

"They did. They have, in fact, been quite vocal on your behalf."

"They have?"

He nodded, a pleased grin on his face. "I get the feeling that they're getting their revenge on those who've wronged them."

"You mean the dead people."

Rudy stopped at Michael's side, dropping my clothes on the bed. They both stared down at me, intent.

"Meg, every person who died meant you harm," Michael said carefully.

"So you're saying they died for me."

He scowled. "I'm saying that they were a danger to your life. If they hadn't been killed, they would have killed you."

I looked at Rudy. "So they had to die."

He nodded.

I shook my head, squinching my eyes shut. "Please let this be over."

Michael's hand closed around my forearm, pulling me toward the edge of the bed. "Come. Get dressed and we'll take you downstairs. It looks like the tribunal will conclude tonight."

I edged toward him and folded my legs over the side of the bed. "That fast?"

Michael helped me to my feet, steadying me when I wobbled. "That fast."

Rudy knelt, holding a pair of khakis for me to step into. No panties. His preference, not really mine. I wasn't in the mood to insist.

Michael continued. "They've talked to everyone here except you, including the enforcers. Everything points to you as the innocent party."

Rudy fastened the pants, and they sat me down.

"Really?"

Michael pulled off the T-shirt. "Really."

Rudy held out a bra for me to stick my arms through.

"What about Roland's death?"

"Melissa, Deidre, and Chloe had some interesting things to say about that. Judging from their testimony, he planned to more than just drain you. He was going to own you. He planned to tie your powers so closely to his that he could use them as his own. What they saw was you reflecting his spell back on him. From their description, it was an accident that happened while you were trying to defend yourself."

I gasped and not because Rudy crawled around behind me to fasten my bra. "But do they know about..." I trailed off, not wanting to say.

Michael smiled. "They say they told their story to Shannon and it was Shannon who said that most of his powers probably did drain off into you."

"Shit, then..."

"But she also said that you couldn't have possibly controlled it. The reversal of the spell was an accident."

"It wasn't," I muttered.

Michael squatted down before me, eyes on mine. "Wasn't it?"

Was it? Goddess, I was so out of it that night, maybe I hadn't been in control.

"What did the tribunal say?"

"They haven't yet."

Rudy slid a plain white shirt onto my arms and crawled around to button it while Michael put on my Keds.

"I feel like an invalid."

"T.C. says you'll probably be weak for at least a few days," Rudy told me as he worked. He smiled. "Good thing you've got us to take care of you."

I reached up to smooth his hair. "Yeah. Good thing."

He kissed me quickly, then backed off the bed.

Michael took my hand and pulled me to my feet.

I wobbled again. "I'm not going to make it."

Michael didn't even bat an eye. He bent down and took me in his arms.

The three tribunal members sat on one long side of the dining room table. Each one had at least two aides behind them, and about a dozen shifters lined three walls of the wood-paneled room. A few enforcers—among them Jake Tearney and his buddy—guarded the hallway and the living room.

Michael set me down in the seat in the middle of the table across from the grand leaders. Then he and Rudy took up their places right behind my chair.

"How do you feel, dear?" The portly, dusky-skinned woman smiling at me from directly across the table had to be Sandra Mendez, the grand dame of Central Mexico. Her accent was prominent, but her English was quite clear.

I nodded. "Tired, but I'm all right. Thank you for your spirit healer's help."

She smiled. "Tom is a good healer. He's told us of how you were drained." Her smile faded and she shook her head. "What an awful experience."

I wasn't fooled by the motherly exterior. This woman was sharp as a tack. But I did take heart that her own healer had testified that I'd been drained. It lent credence to the self-defense.

"Margaret."

I turned to face the silver-haired man to Grand Dame Mendez's right. His shining black goatee was at odds with the silver of his neatly coiffed hair. Piercing blue eyes didn't smile at me, but neither did they scowl. This must be Jack Kamski of Eastern Canada. "We'll ask once." His eyes bore into mine. "Did you kill Roland Parks in self-defense?"

What an odd way to ask. Like he was leading me to the answer. Was he? "Yes, Grand Wizard."

"An' dis is why you've gained such tremendous powa'?"

I turned to the woman on Grand Dame Mendez's left. Marie Mercier of the Mid-South United States could have been Marie Laveau, the famed voodoo queen. At least, that's how I'd picture her. A statuesque Creole woman with knowing gray eyes and shining black cornrows that draped her shoulders and full breasts. Both body and head were wrapped in colorful scarves of primarily purple. Her full lips curved into a warm smile for me.

Again, I thought the way she asked was weird. "I imagine so. I-I'm not quite sure how it happened."

Grand Dame Mendez nodded. "Not surprising. Even a grand dame's daughter would find herself overwhelmed with another witch's power." Her eyes flicked up and to my right, landing on Michael. "Luckily, you had two loyal shifters at your call."

Mention of my mother and an admiring look for my unique shifter. Oh, crap, I was beginning to realize what was going on here.

Grand Dame Mendez's brown eyes dropped back to mine. "You are a lucky *chica*."

I nodded acknowledgement.

"We are inclined to believe your claims," Grand Wizard Kamski spoke up again. "But this situation has created quite a mess. We wonder if we could rely on you to help?"

"Help, Grand Wizard?"

He folded his hands on the table before him. "There is a large amount of unstable energy in this house. We have all felt it during our time here, and it is all keyed to you. This tribunal and the Witches' Council would appreciate it if you and your shifters would stay in this house and deal with the situation."

I blinked. "Deal...?"

He nodded. "Either quell it or tame it. Roland Parks created an unsuitable environment for fledgling witches and innocent mundanes. That needs to be rectified."

"Y-you want me to stay in this house?"

"Is that a hardship? You are, after all, one of the benefactors of Mr. Parks's will."

"I didn't know about that before all this started."

He nodded. "We are aware of that, but the fact remains."

I felt myself start to hyperventilate and tried really hard to steady my breathing. "I don't think I know how to stabilize an environment."

"Oh, don't worry, *pica chica*," cooed Grand Dame Mendez. "Help is sure available. *Senhor* Sandoval, as one of the late Alessandro D'Cruz's shifters, must be familiar with such things." Her gaze flicked to him. "Are you not?" I glanced up to see his steady gaze on her. "I am, *senhora*."

He was?!

"Howard Cook can also provide any legal or shifter assistance you might require."

"And you fada has come to help, as well."

"My…"

At a nod from Grand Dame Mercier, one of the shifters stuck his head into the kitchen. A moment later, my father, Julian Newland, strode through the door. He was a tall, gaunt man with chocolate-brown skin and a smile you never knew if you could trust. He was dressed in casual pants and a long-sleeved polo, but his carriage always made him look like he was dressed in an expensive Italian suit. At least to me. He turned that smile on me as he rounded the table. "Hello, daughter." Somewhere, long before I was born, he'd lost almost all trace of his Jamaican-born accent.

I tipped my head to accept his kiss, but didn't rise. Truthfully, I couldn't, still too weak. But I wasn't sure if I'd do it if I could. "Daddy." Despite the fact that he hadn't raised me, both he and my mother insisted I call him that.

"So, Margaret," said Grand Wizard Kamski, "will you help in this dilemma?"

I gulped. "I-I don't see how I could refuse."

Three pleased smiles met me from across the table. Obviously, they didn't see how I could, either.

Michael carried me back up the staircase. I peeked over his shoulder to see Marie Mercier emerge in the hallway with her entourage, clearly in preparation of leaving. Once they'd secured my word that I'd stay, the tribunal had closed.

Fast.

Rudy opened the bedroom door for us, and Michael set me carefully on the bed. Rudy knelt at my feet, taking off my Keds. Michael closed the door behind us and came to sit on the edge of the bed.

I flopped back on the covers, covering my eyes with my arm.

Rudy finished with my shoes and crawled up on the bed beside me. I felt his hand on my belly, stroking light, soothing circles.

I sighed. "Now what?"

There was a pause before Michael answered. "We'll need to send movers out to our house and yours."

I grimaced, sliding my arm until I could cover my eyes with my hand. "Goddess. Is this really happening?"

"Yes."

"I don't want to live here, Michael."

"We can redecorate."

"That's not the point."

"I know."

"They can't make me live here."

"No." But his tone told it all. They couldn't make me, but yet, they had.

"You have experience calming unstable environments?"

A ghost of a smile touched his lips. "There were quite a number of them in Brazil. I don't think anyone ever proved that Alessandro was to blame, but he certainly was the one who cleaned them up. It's a long process, but I know the mechanics."

I frowned at him. "Do I even want you to clarify that?"

He shook his head. "No."

"Goddess, what a mess."

"Oh, come on, Meg," Rudy chided. "It's not so bad. At least you're not on trial for murder anymore."

"Don't let them fool you, Rudy. They still suspect me. They just don't really want to prove it."

"Huh?"

"They're intrigued." I lowered my arm and looked to Michael for confirmation. "There's too much that's happened that they don't know about. They're better off having me here, alive and under surveillance. Am I right?"

Michael shrugged. "Likely, yes. Aside from the fact that it just looks bad that the grand dame tried to kill you and usurp your power."

I heard Rudy growl and felt his hand clench on my belly.

"What?"

His eyes were stark. "You almost died."

I blinked at him, anger and frustration bleeding away in the face of his...fear. "Rudy."

He shoved to hands and knees, then crawled over me. He leaned in and ghosted his lips over the tip of my nose, his eyes closing. "You almost died." His voice cracked. "I felt you slipping away. Goddess, Meg, please let me hold you. I've got to convince myself that you're alive."

This was Rudy. This was my Rudy. This was a man I hadn't even known a month ago, and now he was as much a part of me as my heart. He *was* my heart.

I tipped my chin up, tilting my head just enough so that our lips met.

He hovered, just lips on lips for an endless moment before he fell on me. "Meg!" His arms gathered me up, a hand coming up to support my head as he tore into my mouth, devouring me.

Still weak, I couldn't give as good as I got, but I didn't hold back and I denied him nothing.

He tore his lips from mine finally and dropped me back to the bed. Eagerly, he crawled down my body, attacking my shirt.

A second set of hands appeared to help with the shirt as he parted it. Michael dragged the shirt out from under me as Rudy nuzzled the cleavage pushed up by my bra. When Michael reached under me to unfasten the bra, Rudy shimmied down farther to take care of my pants.

I looked up at Michael as he brought the bra up my arms and off my body. Beautiful, commanding Michael. His green eyes bore into mine, but he said nothing. Slowly, he bent toward my face. But I didn't have any hesitation now. No matter what they'd done, they'd done it for me. For us. They were mine, and I couldn't do without them. I reached up and pulled him down, twisting so we could almost kiss properly. He crawled around to my side, hand plumping one of my breasts, pinching the nipple.

Rudy got my pants off and spread my legs. I groaned at the first feel of his hot breath on my sex. Weakness kept me from being as fully prepared as normal, but he seemed more than happy to help "wake me up," so to speak. He went slowly, savoring me like a meal at a fine restaurant. I groaned into Michael's mouth as the ache began building.

"I can't...not so...much," I pleaded. The mind was willing, but the body could only take so much at that point.

Rudy climbed up my body, settling between my thighs. His cock slid inside me in a slow, easy glide that had me wrapping myself around him, whimpering at my own inability to react properly.

"Michael, fuck me," I whispered. "Please." When Rudy started to pull out, I wrapped weak arms and legs around him to stop him. "No, no. Both of you."

Michael met my gaze over Rudy's shoulder. "Meg, are you sure?"

I knew what he was asking. The size of his cock compared to the size of my asshole scared me, but at the moment I needed them both. I nodded.

Rudy eyed me. "We could switch?" Which was more normal. Although he was still rather large, Rudy's cock wasn't as wide as Michael's.

"No. I'm sure." I met Michael's gaze again. "Please?"

He nodded and climbed off the bed to find the lube.

Rudy kissed me softly, sliding in and out of me slowly, taking it easy on me. Building it up.

Michael came up on the bed. Rudy slid into me as far as he could, braced his arms around me, then rolled so that I ended up sprawled over him. Michael knelt behind me. Warm hands slid up my spine, followed by a hot, wet tongue. "Are you sure?" he asked once more when his lips reached the vicinity of my ear.

"I'm sure."

Rudy kept moving beneath me as Michael sat back. I tried to brace on weak arms, but finally gave up and just lay across Rudy's chest. Still holding me, Rudy edged us both higher on the bed until he could prop his back in the pillows against the headboard. This way he was mostly sitting. It put me at a better angle, allowing me to reach up to grab the top of the headboard, gripping it with what little strength I had just as Michael slid a wet finger inside me.

"Oh, yes," I sighed, easing back. Knowing where this was leading, knowing what I asked for, I let go of everything but the headboard, relaxing into my lovers. Trusting them to care for me.

A second finger, then a third worked into me, stretching me as Rudy continued to slowly fuck me. The fingers left me and I knew this was it. Michael was getting himself ready.

Rudy must have seen something in my face. "Meg, you don't have to do this. Not now."

I opened my eyes to meet his gaze, surprised to find tears blurring my vision. Unable to speak what I was feeling, unable to voice my need for this, I released my weak hold on the leashes and let them flow.

Rudy groaned as the emotion that stoppered my throat hit him.

Behind me, I heard Michael echo the groan.

There. Now they felt it. The need to be one.

The blunt head of Michael's cock caressed my anus. Agonizing delight flowed into me as he pushed in, mixing with the pain of entry and changing it to pure brandy delight.

I gasped, head fallen forward, hair trailing over Rudy's chest as Michael worked his way inside me. Rudy rocked his hips to help. It hurt, but Goddess the whole thing was wonderful.

When he was in as far as he could go, Michael paused. Warm, orange-yellow magic surrounded us, so merged that I couldn't tell which were Michael's leashes and which were my own.

Michael took the rhythm, slowly at first, pressing into me as Rudy pulled out. I clutched the headboard, unable to do anything in this tableau but relax and let them guide me.

No, not true. I could do something. I gathered the magic: mine, Michael's, and Roland's. I gathered all I could of what we had and fed the connections between us. My leashes pulsed, surging and pumping more energy through me into Michael. Within him, the power caught a second wind, picking up strength to surge back into me, flowing through Rudy.

Our bodies followed the energy, rocking and flowing as Michael and I exchanged power. I lost track of the physical, adrift in the pure sensation of our connection, of the joy of being together. We rocked and flowed, pounded and gasped, moaned and gave. It was never-ending, spiraling up and up, higher and higher, deeper and deeper until we simply weren't large enough to contain it.

We came in blasts of energy, first Rudy, then Michael. I didn't, but only because my body was too worn out to make it. I shared in their orgasms, and with the energy exchange, it was enough.

Mine, I told myself as we melted into a warm pile. No matter what awaited us, I had no doubts that they were mine.

THE END

Jet Mykles

Jet's been writing sex stories back as far as junior high. Back then, the stories involved her favorite pop icons of the time but she soon extended beyond that realm into making up characters of her own. To this day, she hasn't stopped writing sex, although her knowledge on the subject has vastly improved.

An ardent fan of fantasy and science fiction sagas, Jet prefers to live in a world of imagination where dragons are real, elves are commonplace, vampires are just people with special diets and lycanthropes live next door In her own mind, she's the spunky heroine who gets the best of everyone and always attracts the lean, muscular lads. She aids this fantasy with visuals created through her other obsession: 3D graphic art. In this area, as in writing, Jet's self-taught and thoroughly entranced, and now occasionally uses this art to illustrate her stories, or her stories to expand upon her art.

In real life, Jet is a self-proclaimed hermit, living in southern California with her life partner. She has a bachelor's degree in acting, but her loathing of auditions has kept her out of the limelight. So she turned to computers and currently works in product management for a software company, because even in real life, she can't help but want to create something out of nothing.

Printed in the United States
83645LV00009B/4-33/A